ALSO BY GAR

NOVELS

Silversands
The Recollection
Ack-Ack Macaque
Hive Monkey
Macaque Attack
Embers Of War
Fleet of Knives
Light of Impossible Stars

NOVELLAS

Ragged Alice

COLLECTIONS

The Last Reef
The New Ships

NON-FICTION

About Writing

THE MONSTER DIDN'T DREAM.
At least, he didn't remember dreaming.
He wasn't aware of time passing.
And when he awoke, he was already drowning...

CONTENTS

1.

Lee's father was from Swansea, his mother from London. They were both college lecturers. Even in the holidays, they had work to do, books to read. Having successfully bred once, they seemed disinclined to repeat the experiment. Lacking siblings and scorned as a 'blow-in' by the other children in the village, it was inevitable Lee would wind up in the orbit of another outcast—in this case, the farmer's daughter from the house on the hill.

She lived with her father in the farmhouse at the top of the lane, high above the higgledy terraces of the village. He was an ideological farmer, a city boy driven to the country by a need for self-sufficiency and a fear of urban collapse. Their house had solar panels, a composting toilet, and a wind turbine whose blades rattled as they spun. The cellar held enough tinned food for a year. Growing up readied and prepared for an environmental or political apocalypse, Kerri was as different to the pinch-faced village girls as June is to January. She had six freckles on her nose; comb-resistant tresses of off-blonde hair that danced and played behind her ears; and eyes as bottomless and unreadable as the sky-polished surface of a tarn.

In the summer, when the tractors droned and grumbled in the fields and the high-hedged roads were full of walkers heading for a day's ramble around the brown bracken foothills of the Brecon Beacons, the two of them would sit in the shade of the ruined tower in the paddock to the west of the village, their backs resting against the coolness of the stones. The tower and a few crumbled walls were all that remained of a twelfth century castle and constituted the village's one and only tourist attraction. They scuffed their feet in the dirt, watching newly shorn lambs nose among the fallen stones; read superhero comics; and listened to music on their mobiles. Kerri liked anything with a beat and a bit of aggression. She was also occasionally a bit mean to him and teased him the way girls sometimes do; but she let him hang around with her, and together they explored the hills, her father's farm, and the ruins of the castle.

And then, on one particularly hot and drowsy August afternoon, when they were fourteen years old and stretched out in the shadow of the old tower, she saw a helicopter and burst into tears.

They'd been lying in companionable silence, looking up at the dome of sky suspended between the hills on either side of the valley, and Lee had been thinking about the stars and how they were all still there, on the other side of that blue curtain, and how it was only the fact that they were hidden during the day that let mankind forget what a precarious and insignificant ball it lived on, adrift in a vast eternity of night. How different, he wondered, would we have been as a species if, throughout history, the stars remained visible during the day? Would we have still bothered to raise monuments and build skywards like the builders of this castle tower; or would our spirits have been crushed beneath the weight of the universe? Personally, he rather liked the idea of having that constant reminder. At home, he'd filled his bedroom walls with old Hubble photographs of rosy nebulae and colliding galaxies, and pictures of Mars and Titan torn from the pages of National Geographic. His dream was to one day program his computer with a complete and accurate scale model of the solar system: a simulation he could explore at his leisure, with every comet, rock and asteroid accounted for and in their proper orbits.

He and Kerri both had computers, of course; but where Kerri was content to play games and mess around on the Internet, Lee wanted to know how his worked. At school, while the other kids flocked and clustered, he sat in the corner and read programming manuals and computer magazines. It wasn't enough for him to know how to use the desktop his parents had given him; he wanted to delve into its code and build his own worlds and amusements. Because, he thought, what would be the point of owning such a remarkable machine if you weren't going to pop the hood and tinker with it, and exploit its full potential?

Sometimes, he wondered if he was the only person in the village with a drop of curiosity in his head. He couldn't understand how the people around him could go on ploughing the dreary furrows of their lives when all around them, just beyond the valley's hillsides, the entire universe seethed with drama and potential. On clear nights, he'd sit at his bedroom window and watch the vault of Heaven wheel overhead, and imagine himself as an old man, withered and gnarled; a lone scholar huddled over a lamp in the topmost nook of the castle's tower, custodian of the world's few remaining books of science and literature (and superhero comics); curator of knowledge and learning that would otherwise be lost to the ravages of the weather, and the indifference of the barbarians outside.

He was about to open his mouth to ask Kerri if she ever thought about the stars during the day, when he heard the eggbeater thump of an approaching helicopter, and a grey military transport chopper battered its way down the length of the valley, sashaying from side to side as it tracked the course of the river that wound across the valley's meandering floor. He and Kerri watched it pass overhead; so low they could read the number painted on its underside and feel the thud-thud-thud of its rotors in their chests.

Lee sat up to watch it clatter off down the valley. When he turned to Kerri, he saw that tears were sliding down her cheeks in translucent stripes.

"What is it? What's the matter?"

She let her gaze fall from the dwindling helicopter and angrily wiped her eyes on the back of her wrist.

"Shut up."

"But-"

"You wouldn't understand." She turned away and sniffed.

Lee glanced nervously around the paddock. "Are you okay?"

Kerri pulled a crumpled tissue from the pocket of her denim shorts and snuffled wetly into it. "I heard about Mike, okay?" she said.

Lee blinked, then frowned. "Mike?"

Kerri gave him a look. "Mike James. You know, Glyn's older cousin. He lived with his ma on Forest Street."

"Oh, him." Lee remembered the kid as a red-haired, thick-knuckled bully, maybe four or five years older than them. "Didn't he join the army?"

Kerri climbed to her feet. In the week since the start of the school holidays, the sun had tanned her scrawny legs the colour of weak tea. She brushed grass from her palms.

"Yeah, and now he's dead." Her lips whitened as she pressed them together. Then her face collapsed like a sagging cake and she stood there, hands at her sides, sobbing.

Lee scrambled up. His heart thumped with an odd sort of panic. He didn't know what to say. He wasn't used to girls crying. Tentatively, he reached out and touched her shoulder. "What happened?"

"H-he was in Afghanistan and he d-died."

"How?"

Angrily, she brushed a strand of hair away from her eyes. "Does it matter?"

Lee withdrew his hand and used it to adjust his glasses. "I don't understand why you're so upset."

Kerri hunched her shoulders. "I've never known anyone who died before."

"But he was a dick."

"That doesn't mean he deserved to die!" She crossed her arms over her chest and walked away. Lee watched her go.

He could feel the sun on the back of his neck. The air held the farmyard scents of scorched grass and sun-warmed dung, and his insides felt empty, hollowed out by an inexplicable sense of aching loss.

He didn't see Kerri for the whole of the next week. She wouldn't answer her phone or reply to his texts. When she finally came to find him, he was surprised at how much she'd changed. She'd chopped her tangled locks into a Warhol mop, and wore a denim jacket at least three sizes too large. A pair of sunglasses perched on the end of her nose. The small, round lenses shimmered with the iridescent peacock sheen of an oily puddle.

"Where have you been?"

A shrug.

They were standing by the tower, in their usual spot. She pulled a soft pack of cigarettes from the jacket and tapped one out.

"When did you start smoking?"

She pushed the cigarette between her lips and pulled out a disposable plastic lighter.

"You don't know everything about me." Her thumb clicked the little wheel and, with her hands almost imperceptibly trembling, she held the flame up to the cigarette's tip.

As she sucked the cigarette into life, Lee watched the smoke curl around her face and hair, grey and blue in the sunlight. He could feel his heart twitching in his chest, panicky with the sense that he was witnessing an act of perverse and irreversible self-mutilation.

Kerri looked over her glasses at him and smiled. Then she offered him the pack.

"Do you want one?" She waggled it, daring him.

Lee shook his head. "No way."

"God," she laughed, "you're so immature."

She leant her denim shoulders against the stone tower and crossed her legs at the ankle.

Lee looked down at his clothes. He wore a red superhero t-shirt and a pair of knee-length cargo shorts that his mother had bought him. He felt his cheeks flush. Kerri was right; he was still a kid. And, at some point over the past week, she'd become something else. She'd gone on without him, leaving him behind. The little girl he'd known had left, displaced by something taller and leaner, with awkward, self-conscious limbs and eyes that glittered with an aggrieved and surly hunger. He swallowed hard. A pair of bright white butterflies danced between the fallen stones like scraps of windblown paper. A lorry ground its gears on the main road out of town.

"So, what do you want to do?" he asked, struggling to keep his voice level. Kerri looked at him. Then she pulled out her mobile and started thumbing through her text messages.

"You do what you like. I'm waiting for someone."

"Who?"

She huffed, exasperated by his questions. "Him."

Lee turned to see Glyn James, Pete Evans and Geraint Hughes climbing over the stile at the village end of the paddock. Like Kerri, the three boys held their cigarettes curled self-consciously in their hands. They spat the smoke from the corners of their mouths like curses. "Oh shit. What do they want?"

"Glyn probably wants his jacket back."

Lee looked at her with wide eyes. "You nicked it?"

Kerri laughed. "No, he lent it me. He says he's taking me to the disco at the church hall tonight."

"But, but," Lee waved his arms, lost for words. Glyn James was in the year above them at school. When he wasn't playing football, he was finding new and inventive ways to make their lives a misery. "He's a dick."

Kerri's eyes narrowed into slits. "You said that about his cousin. Maybe you'd like to see him dead, too?"

"I never said that."

"You didn't have to."

Lee felt his eyes prickle. "Why are you being like this?"

With a shrug of her shoulders, Kerri pushed herself away from the castle wall. "Like what?"

"I don't know." He waved a hand. "Different."

"You wouldn't understand; you're too immature." Angrily, she tugged at her cuffs. Then she turned to face the approaching boys. "All right, Glyn? What's happening?"

Glyn took a last drag on his cigarette, and then flicked the butt into the weeds. He spoke around a mouthful of smoke. "You coming up the hill?"

Kerri swallowed. "Yeah."

"Good." He turned to Lee, and his lip curled. "Hey, *pidyn*," he growled, "keep away from her, yeah?"

Kerri tugged his sleeve. "Ah, leave him alone, Glyn, he's not so bad."

Glyn shook her off. "I don't like him. He's always hanging around." He held his fist in the younger boy's face. "Go on, fuck off. We're going up the hill, see. And we don't want you following us." A finger jab to the chest. "Got that?"

Lee knew enough local slang to know that 'going up the hill' meant they were heading for the old quarry. It was the place the older kids went to snog and fumble. Porn mags, old syringes and used condoms carpeted the floor of the rusty corrugated iron shed at the far end, in the shadow of the rock face. He stuck out his chin. "I can go where I want."

For a moment, the older boy looked surprised by his defiance. Then he shoved him hard against the tower's stones and slapped him across the face. Lee's glasses fell to the floor.

Glyn drew his fist back, ready to throw a punch, but Kerri caught his wrist. She pulled him away. "Come on, you said you'd leave him alone if I did what you wanted."

Glyn shook her off. He ran a hand across his hair and looked her up and down. Then he smirked. "All right, then."

Lee knelt to retrieve his specs.

As he cleaned them on his t-shirt and slid them back onto his nose, Kerri led Glyn across the field to the lane. The other two boys slouched along behind, grinning at each other around their cigarettes. Occasionally, one or the other would turn and flip Lee an obscene gesture.

Miserably, he watched them go. His fists were knotted at his sides. His throat felt tight and his eyes were burning. His face stung where he'd been hit. Mercifully, he managed to wait until they were out of the paddock before he started to cry.

He didn't want to follow them. He knew no good could come of it, yet he couldn't help himself. Tears rolling down his cheeks and fogging his glasses, he stumbled forward on traitorous feet, unwilling and yet somehow compelled. With each step, he winced, cringing inside at the prospect of the hurt to come; but still he trudged onward, inexorably drawn to the lip of the quarry by a slow gravitational inevitability.

Instead of following the lane and risking a beating at the hands of Pete and Geraint, he took the steep, rocky path that followed one of the streams up onto the hills and looped around to the top of the quarry.

The quarry itself was a deep bowl-shaped depression scooped from the hill's flank. Its sides were steep slopes of scree tangled with brambles, brown, tinder-dry bracken, and yellow-flowering gorse. When he reached the edge, he dropped to his stomach and wriggled forward. From up here, he could see everything, from the old black gates with their desultory curls of barbed wire, to the rust-red roof of the corrugated iron shed. Bees droned back and forth on incomprehensible errands. An old, burned-out car lay swamped in a patch of nettles, the glass long-gone from its windows, fading layers of graffiti carved into its paintwork and sprayed across its roof and bonnet. It all lay spread before him, pinned and sweltering beneath the weight of the hot, still air.

Kerri stood by the door of the shack. She'd taken off the borrowed jacket, and it lay draped over a rock. Her sunglasses were still in place, and she had a cigarette dangling from her teeth. Glyn stood in the doorway. His two lieutenants, having been dismissed by their leader, were in the process of sauntering back down the lane in search of fresh mischief. As Lee watched, Glyn circled Kerri's waist with his slab-like hands and bent to plant his lips against her throat.

Lee felt that kiss like a rail spike to his chest. His eyes filled with tears, and he dropped his forehead onto his arms. He'd thought they were friends and comrades. How could she have gone over to the enemy and so thoroughly betrayed him?

He lay there for a while, immobilised by his dejection. He couldn't watch, but neither could he bring himself to leave. Down in the valley, the village huddled around its ruined castle. He thought of running for help, but whom in that ill-disposed encampment would he ask? He had no other friends. His parents were both at their respective jobs, and Kerri's father was at work in his fields on the opposite side of the valley. If he tried to reach any of them, whatever was going to happen in the quarry would be long over by the time they could get here. There was, he realised for the first time in his life, nobody who could help him. Never had he felt so completely and wretchedly alone.

Without wanting to, he looked back down into the quarry. Glyn had his right hand on Kerri's t-shirt, cupping her left breast. His other hand gripped her upper arm. He whispered something in her ear, and then stepped back, pulling her into the shadowy interior of the corrugated iron hut.

No!

Tears ran down Lee's face. He clenched his fists and drummed his feet against the grass. He took his glasses off and rubbed his eyes with his knuckles.

How could this be happening?

He rolled onto his back and looked up at the blue vault of the sky. The air seemed to shimmer with the heat. Flies and other insects buzzed back and forth. Unbidden, his mind filled with obscene imaginings, and he held his fists to his head and moaned. He felt hot and sick and sweaty, and his guts seemed to be squirming around with a life of their own. He knew with a clear and anguished certainty that, after this afternoon, nothing would ever be quite the same. A threshold had been irrevocably breached and there would be, and could never be, any turning back.

Lee heard laughter coming from inside the hut. Urgent whispers. The unzipping of clothes. Without knowing quite how or why, he found himself standing at the top of the steep scree slope with a rock in his hand. "Stop it!"

His hand whipped around, sending the rock arcing down into the quarry. With appalled fascination, he watched it fall towards the hut's iron roof.

Clang!

The sounds stopped. Lee swallowed but stood his ground. Red-faced, Glyn came running out into the light. He had his shirt off and his jeans were hanging open. He held them up with one hand while using the other to shade his eyes.

"You!" He shook his fist at Lee. "You little bastard. Just you wait 'till I get up there."

"Leave her alone!"

"Or what?" The older boy zipped and buckled his jeans. "What are you going to do, throw stones?"

Behind him, Kerri appeared in the doorway. Her sunglasses were missing. She held her blouse closed. Her skin looked cold and white in the sunlight.

Glyn turned to her. "Get back in there."

"You leave him alone."

She tried to push past, but he blocked her way. "Go on, get back inside."

Glyn was a good head taller than her. He reached big hands for her shoulders but with a laugh, Kerri skipped back through the doorway.

"Go home, Lee," she called. "I'm all right. Everything's fine."

Lee felt himself flush with heat. He could hear the laughter in her voice. His palms prickled. Without thinking, he scooped up another, bigger rock, and threw it with all his strength.

As soon as it left his fingers, he saw its trajectory, inevitable and unstoppable. It was a black asteroid tumbling through empty space, moving with infinite slowness. Lee felt his blood pulse in his ears once.

Twice.

Three times.

Intent on following Kerri, Glyn, perhaps warned by some tingling instinct, glanced up.

The rock caught him across the bridge of the nose. The thump of the impact seemed to echo off the hills. The force of it snapped his head back on his neck. For a long, sickening moment, he remained standing, face raised to the sky, mouth open. Then he fell to his knees, and then onto his front. His jaw hit the dirt floor with a crack and his head lolled over to the side. His legs shook once and were still.

•

Kerri came up the slope. She was fastening her jeans and zipping her jacket. Straightening her spiky hair. She put her hands on either side of Lee's face, and her eyes burrowed into his. First one, then the other, as if somewhere in the black mirrors of his pupils she might find an answer that made sense of what had just happened. Her fingertips were like talons against his scalp. Then, with a cry of exasperation, she let go and flopped down beside him. He watched her light a cigarette.

"Nobody ever finds out about this," she said, speaking around the smoke. Her hands were shaking so hard she could hardly hold her lighter. "Do you understand? You can't tell anybody."

Lee wasn't really listening. He couldn't even feel the sun on his skin. In his head, he was standing on the battlements of the old ruined tower while the world fell apart beneath him. He felt like a husk, as if his insides had been scraped and hollowed by a flint axe, and his skin wrapped and sewn around the resulting void.

Everything was wrong.

He had become one of the barbarians.

2.

When Lee turned eighteen, he escaped to college. He packed up his comic collection and keyboard, and went to study computer science at Bristol University, where his fellow students often mistook his introversion for aloofness. He lost touch with Kerri, who'd fled to start a new life in Manchester. He wore a different superhero t-shirt every day, and let his hair grow shaggy and unkempt.

After graduation, he got a job with a software development company based in a warehouse redevelopment by the docks. Rather than return home to his small border town, he'd decided to stay in Bristol. He moved into a Victorian town house in the Hotwells area of the city, which he shared with three of his co-workers. Situated halfway up one of the steep terraced streets behind the Mardyke pub, the house had a patio area at the rear that overlooked part of the harbour. Lee took the attic room on the fourth floor, which was linked to the rest of the house by a precipitous and winding wooden staircase. From the window, he could see into the gardens of the neighbouring houses, and right across the patchwork rooftops of south Bristol to the sinuous curves of Dundry Hill and the planes lowering on their approaches to the airport. He had his bed on one side of the room, his desk and computer on the other. A fading spider plant stood in a pot on the windowsill. Software manuals and superhero comics filled the bookshelves beside the desk. Newspapers and gaming magazines lay stacked on the carpet beside the door in gently subsiding piles. The Led Zeppelin poster pinned to the back of the door had been there when he moved in. This was the highest room in the house, and it was his sanctuary - a tower from which he could look out at night and see the barbarians going hither and thither about their business.

In August, a couple of months after moving into the house, he found out that his parents were going through a divorce. His mother phoned one wet and thundery Sunday afternoon to tell him. His father, always vague and distant and never really suited to a life beyond the confines of his own research, had apparently taken up with his assistant, a student from Wyoming.

"Of course, she's younger than you." Through the receiver, his mother's voice sounded weary and distant, and stripped of its usual bite. "But what really bothers me is that I welcomed her into my house. Time after time, she sat at my table and ate my food. Supposedly she was helping your father with his book. At least, that's what they said they were doing."

Lee stood by the window, holding the phone to his ear, watching raindrops spot and slither on the glass. The weight of the rain seemed to bow the city, bending over its streetlamps and sagging its roofs.

"Mum, I'm sure-"

"Not that I blame him, of course. Not really. He and I haven't been getting along sexually for years. Not since you were born. And now that you've left home, I guess there's no reason for either of us to keep pretending we're happy."

"So, it's my fault?"

"Not at all, darling. You mustn't think that. I just wish he'd been open about it instead of skulking around behind my back like a furtive teenager."

Lee switched the phone to his other ear. Floorboards creaked and pipes clanked in the wall as one of his housemates ran the hot tap in the communal bathroom.

"Where's Dad now?"

"He's gone. He packed a suitcase and left. I think he's staying at her place."

"What about his books?"

"He says he doesn't need them. He left his job at the University and says he's going to become an artist, if you can believe that. They both are."

Lee closed his eyes.

When he reopened them, the sky was dark and the phone dead in his hand. He had no idea how much time had passed. The window opened onto a flat section of roof, maybe a metre wide. He climbed out and stood there in the drifting rain, looking towards the orange lights of the city centre. Lightning danced on the horizon. At the bottom of the hill, a police armed response van cruised the main street.

Protective metal grilles covered its headlights and windscreen, and its bodywork looked black and solid against the gaudy reds and blues of the kebab shops and taxi offices. The rain ran down his cheeks and dripped from his nose and chin. Four storeys below, the patio's crazy paving lay black and slick, and encrusted with weeds like the skin of a mythical sea kraken.

Thunder grumbled and rolled.

All it would take would be one step...

He raised his face to the sky, imagining the Universe beyond the orange, glowering clouds. Lightning flashed again, closer this time. All the hairs stood up on his arms.

His childhood memories were as remote as a picnic scene on the far side of a wide river, glimpsed through a willow's tresses: bright, but unreachably distant. He felt like a husk, as if his insides had been scraped and hollowed by a flint axe, and his skin wrapped and sewn around the resulting void.

They say we're the sum of our memories, he thought. *That our remembrances shape our personalities—but what happens to us when we forget something?*

The thunder boomed again, so boisterously loud that he felt the sound shake his lungs and diaphragm.

When our memories are lost or taken from us, what remains?

Hail pattered onto the tiles behind him.

Who do we become?

•

The next morning, he woke fully clothed on his bed. He'd left the window open. The sill was wet with rain, but the storm itself had passed. From where he lay, he could see a silver vapour trail high in the crisp morning sky. The summer air smelled of hibiscus and damp earth.

He got up and showered and changed into a fresh t-shirt. Then he set off on the fifteen-minute walk along the harbourside to his office. Gulls wheeled in the air. Yellow-painted ferries chugged back and forth, the sun dancing off the waves pushed up by their bows.

He passed the remains of a beer bottle, which lay smashed in the gutter by the bus stop. On the wall of the newsagents on the corner next his office, an unseen hand had spray-painted 'life goes wrong' in wobbly pink letters.

The warehouse that accommodated his office had originally been built for the tea trade in the 1830s. It had lain fallow for some years as the port declined but had then been reborn in the building boom at the start of the Millennium. Pushing through the main glass doors into the pine-floored reception area, he eschewed the open cage-like elevator in favour of a black wrought-iron spiral stair and pulled himself up to the second floor.

Its founders had named Green Sphinx Enterprises after a breed of moth and used a stylised rendition of the insect as its logo. GSE, as its staff called it, was a medium-sized software provider employing somewhere in the region of fifty people and turning over just under five million pounds per year. Its CEO was an accountant-turned-entrepreneur in his early forties named Dave, who was all smiles and hair products, and whose left ear bore a single platinum stud.

Each employee had his or her own ergonomically curved pine-coloured desk. They were arranged in groups of four, all facing inwards so that everybody was looking at the back of everybody else's monitors. Cardboard coffee cups, old pens, cracked rubber stress toys and other detritus accumulated in the no-man's land at the centre, around the holes at the back of each desk into which the phone and power cables vanished.

Lee's desk was at the back of the room, and his chair was sandwiched between it and the rear brick wall. While the other employees jostled for positions closer to the windows at front of the building, he'd staked this one as his own because it was the only one in the room at which he could be sure no- one was looking over his shoulder. No one could sneak up on him here, and nobody could see what it was he was doing.

He'd stacked software manuals and ring binders on either side of his monitor, and superhero action figures stood guard beside his keyboard. He drank his coffee from a NASA mug and all his notes were written into a black, hardcover notebook.

This early in the day, few of his co-workers were in evidence. They tended to drift in mid-morning and work until nine or ten at night, so he had the place pretty much to himself, which usually meant he'd spend an hour or so working on his secret project, the space simulation he'd been dreaming about since he was fourteen. This morning, however, he couldn't bring himself to open the file. All his enthusiasm for the project had gone and the whole idea seemed suddenly childish and self-indulgent. Instead, he sat there staring into the middle distance. He was twenty-two years old and he felt like an orphan.

By midday, he hadn't achieved anything remotely productive. He couldn't concentrate on his work, so he decided to walk to the café at the end of the street to buy a sandwich. He wasn't really hungry, but he hoped the fresh air might clear his head. He got up from his desk, mumbled something to his supervisor, and took the lift down to the ground floor.

When the lift reached reception and the doors opened, he saw Kerri waiting for him. Her eyes were lowered to the heavy-looking shoulder bag at her feet. Her teeth chewed her bottom lip. For a moment, all he could do was stand and gape, drinking her in. Then the doors began to close, and he had to put out a hand to stop them.

"Kerri?" He cleared his throat. "Oh my God. What are you doing here?"

Her head jerked up. She stood straighter and wiped her eyes on the cuff of her denim jacket. "Take me for a drink," she said.

•

Lee took her to The Lion, a small corner pub close to his house, and the nearest thing he had to a local. By the time they got there, all evidence of tears had vanished from her eyes. They ordered drinks—a bottle of Spanish lager for him; a vodka and coke for her—and took them out to a table in the beer garden.

"So," she said, placing her bag on the concrete floor at her feet, "how's the job?"

Lee looked at her. She was four years older than she had been the last time they'd seen each other, and she'd lost some weight around her face. Her cheeks seemed thinner and the shadows deeper beneath her eyes.

"Okay, I guess." They had the garden to themselves. "You don't sound very enthused."

"Well, it's hardly my dream job."

"What is it you do?"

Lee sipped the froth from the top of his bottle. It tasted vaguely coppery. "I write code."

"For computer games?"

"No, but I wish I did. At least that would be interesting."

"What, then?"

"We provide ERP systems designed for small and medium-sized organisations."

"ERP?"

"Enterprise Resource Planning. It's basically an accounts package with bolt-on HR and payroll modules."

"Sounds riveting."

"Trust me, it's not." They lapsed into an awkward silence. The 'garden' was little more than a repurposed and high-walled yard. Kerri fiddled with the button on the cuff of her denim jacket. Eventually, and without looking up, she asked,

"Do you ever go back?"

"What, back home?" Lee shook his head. His fingers worried the label on his beer bottle. "My parents are getting a divorce." It was the first time he'd said it out loud.

"Oh shit, I'm sorry."

"I guess these things happen. At least, they happen to other people all the time. I just never expected..." He trailed off. In his mind's eye, he saw a stone tumbling through the hot and empty air above the sun-bleached quarry. In the past eight years, neither of them had mentioned Glyn but the boy's presence had always been there, in the silences between their words.

"There's nothing back there for me, either." Kerri shrugged matter-of- factly. "Not since Dad sold the farm."

"Where is he now?"

"Living in a teepee in West Wales."

"Really?'

"Yeah." She made a face. "I couldn't believe it either. I was all like, 'you fucking what?' But then he sent me half the money from the sale of the house, which was pretty cool of him, and it got me out of a tonne of shit with my landlord."

"So, what brings you to Bristol?"

Kerri went quiet. After a couple of minutes, she said, "I just broke up with someone. We were living together but things turned weird. I had a job in a sandwich shop near the station and after we broke up, she started hanging out in front of the place, looking through the windows. Sometimes she'd be there for my whole shift, standing in the rain with her face pressed up to the glass."

"So, you left?"

With the toe of her boot, Kerri nudged the bag at her feet. "I had to. I thought she was going to go all Single White Female on me."

"What are you going to do?"

"I don't know. I thought-"

"You want to stay with me?"

"For a few days, if that's okay? I've got nowhere else, really, and you're my oldest friend."

Lee drained his glass, sucking down the last of the suds. "Sure, why not? With the day I've had, I could probably use the company." He looked at the pale curve of her throat. "But I've only got the one bed..."

"I'll be fine on the floor."

"Okay." He looked at the time on his mobile phone. "I've got to be back at work in half an hour. Take my key and make yourself at home. I'll be back just after six."

"Thank you." From the pocket of her jacket she pulled a couple of hand rolled cigarettes. They were a little bent and crumpled, so she smoothed them out on the table's sun-warmed wood. "Here you go." She passed one across to him.

"I don't smoke."

"It's a joint."

Lee picked it up between thumb and index finger. "You mean cannabis?"

Kerri gave a snort of laughter. "Yes, of course. What's the matter? Haven't you ever...?"

"As a matter of fact, no."

"Really?" Despite the raised eyebrows, he thought he detected something more than surprise in her expression:

admiration, perhaps. "Okay, well there's nothing to it. Just watch me. I'll show you what to do."

•

Back at work, the rest of the afternoon passed in a pleasant, if unproductive, haze. When he got home, he found Kerri asleep on his bed. He kicked off his shoes and lay behind her. Her hair smelled of smoke and pine-scented shampoo, and he could feel the warmth of her skin through her clothes. Gently, he draped an arm over her.

For a moment, she snuggled into his embrace, squirming like a contented cat. Then she stopped and went rigid. "What's going on?"

"Huh?"

She shrugged him off and scrambled away, sitting with her back pressed against the wall. "What do you think you're doing?"

He blinked at her. "I don't know, I thought-"

"Jesus Christ!" She smacked her palms on the covers. "Just because I need your help, that doesn't mean I'm going to sleep with you."

"I didn't think-"

"I mean you of all people-"

"What?"

"I don't-" She rubbed the back of her neck. "I mean, not with boys. Not ever."

"What about the quarry?"

Her expression hardened. "That was the one and only time. An experiment. I thought maybe if I tried it with a boy..." Her voice wavered. "It was stupid, but I didn't know what else to do. And then you... You threw that rock."

Lee felt a pit open in his stomach. "Shit, I'm sorry."

"Don't touch me." She pulled the duvet up to cover herself. "Not like that, not ever, okay?"

3.

Lee walked home from work through the golden haze of a warm September's eve. He'd stayed late to talk to Green Sphinx's contractors in California. They were eight hours behind the UK, but he didn't mind. He'd struck up something of a relationship with a programmer called Francesca, who lived in Pasadena and drove a dinged-up Volkswagen Beetle. They had been working on the same project for the past six weeks, and a few playful comments in their work- related emails to each other had somehow led to some serious flirting on social media. She was a year older than him and liked the same sort of comics he did. She'd just posted a photo of her ankle tattoo to her online profile. Talking to her tonight, even though it had officially been a business call, had been a lot of fun. He couldn't get enough of the way she spoke, and she loved his pronunciation of everyday words. Just saying 'hello' was enough to reduce her to fits of giggles.

"And good day to you, your lordship," she'd reply, putting on her idea of a posh British accent—in reality, an impersonation of Katherine Hepburn's upper-class manner in The Philadelphia Story, which was her favourite movie.

Thinking about her now, Lee smiled. The breeze held the intoxicating scents of hot roads and cool summer evenings. Lawnmowers buzzed behind garden fences, and groups of Friday drinkers milled outside The Lion, listening to the music that came from the open sash windows.

When he reached his front step, he fished out his key and shouldered open the big front door. Kerri was in the communal kitchen, and the aroma of bubbling vegetable curry assailed his nostrils.

"Hey." She had an apron tied around her waist, over a pair of cut-off denim shorts and a black waistcoat. Her feet were bare, and she'd scrunched her hair up in a knot and fixed it in place with a couple of old wooden chopsticks. For the last three months, she'd been living in the basement, which she'd converted into a sort of art studio. She spent most of her time down there, painting these angry black and orange canvasses with titles such as 'Betrayal' and 'Alone in The Void'.

Lee dumped his laptop on the table, walked to the fridge and took out a beer.

"There's a message for you," Kerri said, stirring her pan. She nodded towards the old wooden kitchen table, and its permanent slick of takeaway menus, free newspapers and old phone books. She'd left a handwritten note beneath a used coffee mug. "Somebody called Ali rang. It's about your father."

•

Lee's father lived in Glastonbury, in a red brick terraced house in the shadow of the Tor. It was an hour's drive from Bristol. Coming across the flat wetlands and farm country of the Somerset Levels, the conical hill dominated the skyline. A ruined church tower stood like an ageless monolith on its summit. When Lee knocked at the door of his father's house, Ali opened it.

"Lee?" She was a former art student in her early twenties, all black Lycra, silver bangles and paisley skirts.

"You said it was urgent."

"Yes." She stood aside to let him in. The front room was a mess. As far as Lee knew, they had been in this house for six weeks, yet there were still unpacked boxes stacked against the wall and piles of unsorted books waiting to be shelved. A mobile hung in the corner, twisting gently. It had been made from copper wire, coloured beads and long white feathers. Bare wires above the fireplace showed where the TV would go, when they got around to fixing it up.

"Where is he?"

"Ifan's in his study." Ali fiddled with her necklace. "He really wants to see you."

"Really?" Lee couldn't disguise his resentment. Six weeks had passed since his mother broke the news of the divorce, and his father hadn't been in touch once. The least the old man could have done was pick up the phone to tell his own side of the story, and to check how his son was doing.

"He's in the back bedroom." Ali wouldn't meet his eye. "You go on up, and I'll put the kettle on."

She fled for the kitchen. Lee stood at the bottom of the stairs for a moment. His stomach felt hollow and sour. The coffee he'd drunk on the way here lay inside him like a lukewarm slick.

Suppose the old man had been avoiding him, ducking his disapproval. Why send for him now?

With a huff, Lee gripped the bannister and climbed the creaking staircase. The carpet had been pulled up, revealing the original wooden boards, which were flecked with paint. When he reached the landing, he knocked on the backroom door, and then pushed it open without waiting for a response.

His father sat in an armchair by the window. The view looked out onto the neighbouring gardens. In the sunlight, the hedges and trees seemed almost unbearably green.

"You made it, then?" The old man's voice was gruff. He wore a pair of shabby chinos, a button-down check shirt, and a green corduroy jacket. "How's your mother?"

The only other seat in the room was an office chair by the desk in the corner. Lee pulled it out and eased himself onto it. The casters felt skittish on the bare floorboards.

"Why don't you ask her yourself?" The coffee seemed to be trying to squeeze its way out between his ribs.

"We're not exactly on speaking terms right now."

"And whose fault is that?"

Ifan turned his face to the window. Beyond the garden's rear border, sheep cropped the hillside. "You have a right to be angry."

"Do I?" Lee tapped his toes against the floor. In the car, he'd rehearsed what he was going to say. He'd made a list of grievances, starting with the divorce and working back through his upbringing, numbering all the times his father had been physically or emotionally absent, too caught up in work and research to participate in his own son's childhood, or tend to the wellbeing of his marriage.

"Of course." Ifan didn't turn. "I'm sure you're disappointed at the way things have worked out."

"Disappointed?" Lee stood. The chair rolled away behind him and bumped against the wall. "You don't even know the half of it." He wanted to walk out, get back in his car and go home.

His father sighed.

"Sit down, boy. Before you say anything else, there's something you should know. Something I want to tell you."

Lee's hands were shaking. He squeezed them into fists.

"And what's that, that you feel sorry?"

Ifan shook his head. His chin dropped to his chest. The light from the window picked out the grey in his hair, the dandruff on his shoulders. Downstairs, his girlfriend rattled cups and saucers as she boiled the kettle.

"I'm dying," the old man croaked. "I have cancer."

•

Later, Lee found he was unable to remember leaving the house. The next thing he recalled, he was sitting in the car, in a layby off the A39, somewhere on the Mendip hills between Wells and Bristol. The sun had set, and the sky had turned the colour of a day-old bruise. Ahead, through the windshield, he could see the lights of a plane on approach to Bristol Airport. To the West, above the distant hills of Wales, the clouds smouldered like barbeque coals.

His fingers hurt from gripping the steering wheel, so he pried them loose and opened the door. Outside, an evening breeze flapped his shirt, bringing with it the rural aromas of dried cow shit, warm earth and fresh hay. His arms and legs felt wobbly with shock. From across the fields, he could hear the low grumble of a tractor.

Walking carefully around to the passenger side, he opened the door and looked in the glove box. Kerri had left a couple of joints and a box of matches in a drawstring bag. He retrieved one and, leaning against the car, lit up, cupping his hand around the match to stop it going out. The smoke bit into his chest, but he managed not to cough. He felt his head go light and exhaled gratefully. It was almost ten o'clock. He took another drag and, holding the smoke inside, reached into the car and flipped on the radio. Through the soles of his shoes, he could feel the day's heat oozing from the dusty tarmac. He thought back to the night his mother had telephoned to tell him of the divorce. Had she known then that her husband was dying, that he had less than six months to live? It was all such a ragged, shitty mess, and he couldn't see a way to fix it. His parent's relationship had always been something of a mystery to him. They had never been given to public displays of affection and tended to converse at the breakfast table like academic colleagues rather than lovers. And now, not only had that fragile domestic charade been taken from him, so had all hope of a reconciliation. The doors were finally and irrevocably closing on his childhood. The set had been struck, the props were being taken down and put away, and one of the actors was about to be swept offstage for good.

Lee swore under his breath. He tipped his head back and blew smoke at the cold, eternal stars. Nothing about the situation was fair—not to him, not to his mother, and most especially not to his father—and there wasn't a damn thing he could do about it.

He stood there with the smouldering roll-up dangling unheeded from his fingers, staring blindly at the heavens for some time before he became aware of the shape looming over him. In fact, he realised his eyes had been instinctively tracing its outline for a minute or so before his conscious mind caught up and acknowledged its presence.

"What the hell?" He pushed himself away from the car and frowned. Something was occluding the stars—something black, silent and unreflective, roughly the shape of a rugby ball and approximately the size of an ocean liner. It hung over the road like an unpaid debt.

•

When Lee arrived home, shortly after midnight, he found the door to the garden open, and Kerri nursing a glass of wine on the back doorstep. The night air smelled of rosemary and jasmine, undercut with occasional greasy wafts from the kebab shop down on the main road. A wine bottle stood on the step by her feet, and she had balanced a half-smoked pack of cigarettes on her bare knee. She offered him one, but he shook his head.

"Are you okay?" He could see her eyeliner had been smudged. One of the chopsticks had gone missing from her hair. A few strands had worked their way loose and now curled around her neck and shoulders.

She swirled the wine around in her glass. "I had a fight with Heather."

"Was it serious?"

"The fight or the relationship?" Kerri took a cigarette and pushed the filter between her lips. When Lee shrugged, she said, "It doesn't matter. They're both over."

"I'm sorry."

"Yeah, so am I."

Lee joined her on the step. "Do you want to talk about it?"

"Not really." Kerri pulled a rusty Zippo from her waistcoat pocket and flicked it into life. The yellow flame wobbled in the darkness. "Tell me about your day," she said, talking out of the side of her mouth as she lit her cigarette. "How was your father?"

"He's dying."

She almost choked on the smoke. "Shit, I'm sorry."

Lee reached down and picked up the bottle. There wasn't much wine left in it. He looked questioningly at Kerri.

"Go ahead," she said. "There's another bottle in the fridge."

•

By two o'clock, they were sitting on the dry and dusty lawn, backs and elbows resting against the step, shoulders touching.

"We used to do a lot of this," Kerri murmured. "Do you remember?" Lee could feel a headache building. He rubbed his eyes.

"Drinking?"

"No." She nudged him. "Sitting around. Do you remember the old castle tower?"

"I try not to think about it."

Kerri scrunched her toes in the dry yellow grass. "We were so young."

Lee finished his wine and put the glass aside. They had gone through three bottles between them. "We're hardly decrepit now, grandma."

"You know what I mean." She gave him a gentle shove. "Besides, I've been reliably informed that it's not the age that counts, it's the mileage."

She put her head on his shoulder and they sat in companionable silence for a few minutes.

"You know," Lee said, looking down at his shoes, "something happened to me tonight."

"What, baby?" Kerri's head stayed where it was. She sounded tired. He inhaled through his nose, savouring the smell of the night, the lingering whiff of tobacco from her hair and clothes. "I saw something."

"At your dad's house?"

"On the road." He looked up at the sky, half-expecting to see movement among the gathering clouds. "It was a-"

"I want to get pregnant."

Lee opened and closed his mouth a few times, his train of thought hopelessly derailed. "I'm sorry, what?"

Kerri's face wrinkled. She looked as if she was trying not to cry. "That's what Heather and I were arguing about. I want one, but she doesn't."

"And that's why you split up?"

"Yes." Her eyes brimmed, glittering in the light from the kitchen. She fumbled for a cigarette. Somewhere, at the back of his throat, Lee felt his own tears gathering. Too much had happened. Without thinking, he reached an arm around her shoulders. It was an instinctive gesture born of the need to feel someone in his arms, to comfort his friend and draw solace in return; the simple necessity of physical human contact. Much to his surprise, instead of flinching away, Kerri wriggled in closer, working her shoulder into his armpit. She sniffed loudly and wiped her face against his shirt. Her hair brushed his neck.

"What time is it?" Her voice came out muffled and sniffly.

Lee glanced at his watch. "Two-fifteen."

"We should go to bed."

"I think you're right." He took his arm from her shoulders and she straightened. He helped her up and they stood facing each other on the doorstep. Kerri tugged at the hem of her waistcoat and brushed dust from the seat of her denim shorts. Beyond the garden wall, at the bottom of the hill, the orange streetlights of Bristol filled the night like the campfires of a sleeping army.

"Can I sleep with you?" Her eyes were wide in the darkness, and Lee was sure he'd misheard.

"I beg your pardon?"

She bit her lip and took his hand in hers. "I don't think either of us should be alone tonight."

"You mean you want to sleep in my bed?"

"I mean, shut up." She pulled him into the house and kicked the door closed with her heel. Standing in the kitchen, lit only by the glowing green numbers on the microwave's digital clock, she unbuttoned her waistcoat.

Lee felt his mouth go dry. His stomach growled. "Is this a good idea?"

Kerri shrugged the waistcoat from her shoulders and let it slide down her arms, onto the floor. She stepped forward, grabbed the front of shirt, and kissed him. Her lips were dry and rough and urgent. Her breath felt hot and smoky in his mouth. "I told you to shut up."

4.

When the call came, Lee and Frankie were hiking in the French Alps, under the watchful gaze of two experienced guides. It was their fifth wedding anniversary. For the last hour they had been following a narrow path above a plantation of snow-topped conifers. When the phone shivered against his hip, Lee swapped both his spike-tipped walking poles into his left hand, pulled off his right glove with his teeth, and answered it. "Hello?"

"Lee, it's Joaquin. Can you talk?" Joaquin Bullock was Francesca's brother-in-law, and a project manager at Lone Tower, the software and technology company Lee had built on the back of his success with the Solar System Simulator.

"Joaquin?" Lee's breath steamed in the frozen air. His fingers tingled. He made an apologetic face to Frankie as she pushed her mirrored goggles impatiently to the top of her head. "Jesus," he said, "what time is it over there?"

A year after their wedding, Frankie had convinced him to move back to Pasadena with her, so he could start his company in L.A. rather than Bristol or Cardiff. Now, six months later, he employed over a hundred people. He had an air-conditioned office at the top of the company building with his name stencilled on the glass: Lee Doyle, Founder and CEO.

"A quarter to five."

"What's the problem?"

"It's the Net."

"What about it?" Four years ago, Lone Tower had successfully bid to refurbish the Interplanetary Network, a series of interlinked satellites and relay stations left over from the days when NASA still had budget and ambition. Placed strategically throughout the Solar System, the network had been designed to make it easier for individual probes and expeditions to report back to Earth, allowing them to hook into an existing web rather than carry bulky communications gear of their own.

"It's become unresponsive. There's still traffic on it, but we can't access any signals. It's like we've been locked out."

"Have we been hacked?"

Bullock's fingers pecked at a keyboard. "I've got guys running that scenario at the moment. Initial results indicate not."

"Then it's some kind of fault?"

"I think it's more than that."

Lee huffed into the clear mountain air. His lungs felt like crystal. "Could you be more specific?"

He heard Bullock swallow and clear his throat. "I think the network's started redesigning itself."

"What? How could it even begin to do that?"

There was a pause.

"It's using the self-repair packages," Joaquin Bullock said. Thanks to Lone Tower, each node in the network now had its own cache of nano-scale assembly robots, capable of patching damage caused by radiation, micrometeorite impact or component failure.

"It's upgrading itself." The man sounded on the slippery edge of panic.

"Hey, calm down." Lee spoke through a sudden hurricane of static.

"I can't calm down!" Bullock's voice dipped and echoed through the fuzz, like a transmission from another world. "I'm getting emails now from the big dish at Arecibo. They're locked out too, but they say something's using their telesco-"

The line hissed and crackled.

"Joaquin!"

The phone went dead. Lee cursed and checked the display. No reception.

Standing in the snow, Frankie raised an eyebrow. "Everything okay?"

Lee held the phone for a moment, hoping the signal would return. When it didn't, he slipped the device back into his pocket and pulled on his glove. "I'm not sure. It's Joaquin. I think he's having some kind of meltdown."

Ahead, their two guides waited at the start of the next downhill stretch, where the firebreak cut down through the snow-sagging, ice-dropped boughs of the pine trees to the lower slopes, and the chimney smoke and warm yellow lights of the village.

"Honestly, I don't know why you employ him."

"Because he's married to your sister."

"Ugh." Her face, framed by her hair and the fur edge of her hood, wrinkled in disgust. "Don't remind me."

She dug her poles into the path's crisp, compacted snow. Her boots crunched. Lee hurried to catch up with her. "You're annoyed?'

"I'm fine."

"It was just Joaquin, having one of his flaps."

"I know." She gave him a rueful look. "That's not the point. You promised, no work calls."

"But-"

The ground shook. A rumble came from above. Lee looked up, stupidly expecting to see a freight train bearing down on them. Instead, all he saw was white. He didn't have time to move or cry out. The cresting wave of snow hit him impossibly fast, snatching him away like so much windblown laundry. He couldn't breathe. He didn't know which way was up. The torrent roared like the stampeding herds of God. He got flashes of daylight. He heard, rather than felt, his shinbone snap. And then, as suddenly as it had come upon him, it was over. The snow slowed and settled around him. He felt its weight piling up onto his chest and stomach, pinioning his arms and legs. It covered his face, cold and rough against his nose and cheeks, and he found himself gasping for breath. From somewhere, he remembered that most avalanche-related fatalities occurred after the avalanche had stopped moving. The snow compressed as it slithered to a halt, packing tighter and harder. Trapped beneath it, your prospects for escape were slight. If you weren't rescued quickly, you were likely to succumb to hypothermia, suffocation or the effects of your injuries.

He blinked flakes from his lashes. He knew his leg was broken, although the pain seemed remote and far away. He was more conscious of a penetrating chill, where a ragged spear of splintered bone had ripped through the skin at the front of his shin and buried itself in the surrounding snow.

He shrugged his shoulders, trying to work his arms loose, but succeeded only in dislodging some of the whiteness above him. It fell across his face and he had to shake his head and snort to clear it from his mouth and nose.

"Frankie!" His voice was a hoarse croak. Each exhalation of breath made space for more snow to topple in on top of him, thereby making the next inhalation all the more laborious.

"Frankie, where are you?"

She'd been standing right beside him when the wave hit. Had she survived? Was she buried as well? He struggled against his confinement, cursing. More powder rained down into his eyes and mouth; little crystals of ice fell like showers of diamond dust. At any moment, the drift's entire weight could fall and smother him. Yet he wouldn't—he couldn't—lie still. He had to find his wife. Like a drowning man, every instinct in his body screamed at him to fight and thrash. He didn't care if his efforts brought freedom or hastened his demise; either would be preferable to lying passively, waiting for a cold, lingering death.

5.

Rain fell on London from a sky the colour of bruised fruit. Lee abandoned his car outside the British Museum, telling the driver to wait there for him rather than risk becoming any more ensnared in the confusion surrounding the site of the latest outbreak. The magazine for which Kerri worked had its offices in a narrow street behind Russell Square. With the traffic this bad, he reckoned he'd be better off on foot. Not even the emergency vehicles were getting through. Up ahead, he could see the blue flashing lights of an ambulance trying to push its way through the gridlock, its nearside wheels up on the pavements, siren wailing. The staccato thrum of helicopter rotors echoed between the buildings. Both the police and press were out in force. Turning up the collar of his coat, he made his way through the crowds. Some were hurrying away from the Square, injured and panicked; others were pressing closer, trying to get a look at the thing that had erupted from the magazine's servers. He barged through them all, ignoring their shouts and protests.

The contagion had spread. For the past six months, mini Singularities had been popping up all over the globe. They erupted like flowers, only to wither and die. Nobody really knew how or why, but neither of those questions really mattered right now. Lee had been on his way to Whitehall when the news of this latest eruption broke, and now all he could think of was finding Kerri.

Even after half a year, his shin hurt where it had been broken in the avalanche. The bone had healed but the damned thing still bothered him when the weather turned wet and cold.

Up ahead, the police were trying to cordon off the road. He limped up to the most senior officer he could see—a harassed-looking sergeant with a radio pressed to one ear—and flashed his Downing Street security pass.

"I need to get through."

"You and half of London, mate."

The man's thick build and unspoken, belligerent assumption of superiority were redolent of a young thug called Glyn, standing in a quarry in Wales while bees buzzed, and a girl called Kerri tried to drag him back into a corrugated iron hut.

"No, seriously, the mother of my son's in there."

The sergeant shrugged. Lee's problems were none of his concern. "Sorry, emergency crews only."

Lee felt his fist curl around an imaginary rock.

"Look at this." He flapped the laminated pass under the man's moustache. "Do you know who I am? I'm Lee Doyle, the CEO of Lone Tower Inc. Ever heard of it? I'm over here advising the government on these outbreaks. I know more about what's happening here than you do. Now, are you going to let me past, or do I have to ring the Prime Minister?"

"Now, listen here-"

"I've got her on speed dial." Lee pulled out his mobile. "All I have to do is press this button." It was the purest bluff. He'd never met the woman personally, only consulted with her advisors—the Prime Minister needed to keep some distance between herself and the measures Lee would have to put in place to curb the spread of the contagion—but this cop wouldn't know that, and Downing Street passes weren't handed out to just anybody; and Lee hadn't built his company into a giant corporation without learning a thing or two about the art of bullshit. He hovered his thumb over the keypad and looked the sergeant in the eye. "Now, I'm going to count to three," he growled. "Are you going to cooperate, or do you want to explain yourself to the PM?"

•

Five minutes later, Lee reached the remains of the magazine's office building just as a stretcher team carried Kerri from the rubble. He caught up with them as they were loading her into the back of a waiting ambulance. She was covered in plaster dust.

"Lee?" Her eyes were bloodshot. She kept hacking.

"I'm here." He squeezed her forearm through the red blanket. One of the medics tried to intervene but he waved his security pass at them.

"Government business," he said.

The office block had partially collapsed. Bits of it were ablaze. Fire crews emptied their hoses through broken, soot-stained windows. Somewhere in the depths of the ruin skulked something black and fibrous. Lee could see one of its tentacles twitching feebly. The bodies of the dead were lined up on the opposite pavement, anonymous beneath identical red blankets, waiting to be taken wherever it was that bodies were taken in these circumstances.

Kerri worked her hand free and gripped his fingers. "Lewis."

"What about him?" Lee glanced at the rubble in alarm. "Oh God, he's not in there is he?"

Kerri's lips were dry and cracked; her clothes stank of smoke. "No, he's at home with Heather."

"Thank Christ."

"Lee, listen. If anything happens to me, you have to promise-" She broke into a series of wracking coughs.

"Nothing's going to happen to you." He turned to the waiting medics for confirmation. "Right?"

The stretcher-bearers exchanged a look. "We need to get her to hospital."

"Why, how bad is it?"

"She's inhaled a lot of smoke. At least one broken rib. There may be some internal bleeding."

"Shit. Then I'm coming with you."

He let them load her into the ambulance and climbed in beside the stretcher. He pulled out his mobile phone. "Which hospital are we going to?"

"UCH." The driver turned the key in the ignition. "The rest are swamped."

The wipers clunked back and forth across the windscreen. Lee scrolled through his contacts and selected Kerri's home number. Heather answered on the second ring. She had been watching the catastrophe on the news. He told her where they were going and hung up.

Rain beat on the ambulance roof. Cars choked the roads, and groups of people were gathering on street corners in the rain. The medic slipped an oxygen mask over Kerri's face. A valve hissed every time she exhaled. By the time they reached the hospital, she had stopped breathing altogether. The ambulance crew whisked her into the treatment room. Lee tried to follow but found his way barred by the arm of a stressed-looking nurse. Hands in pockets, he walked back to the overcrowded reception area. When Heather turned up, almost an hour later, it took her a moment to spot him in the crowd.

"Any news?"

He shook his head. He hadn't been able to elicit anything useful from the staff. There were simply too many casualties. Those patients that could be moved were being shipped off to Royal London and St. Thomas's. Minor injuries were being turned away at the door. People infected by the Reef were being moved to a special quarantine facility.

"Where's Lewis?"

"He's with a friend." Heather brushed back her wet hair. Beneath her raincoat, she wore an old rugby shirt and jogging bottoms. A furled umbrella dripped from her left hand. "I didn't want to bring him." She slid the umbrella into her shoulder bag and pushed her hands into her coat pockets. "I was sorry to hear about your wife."

"Thank you."

"You didn't have any children, did you?"

"No." Lee swallowed. "No, we couldn't."

"I'm sorry."

"Yeah, me too." For the first time in years, he found himself wanting a drink or a cigarette. Mostly, he just wanted something to do with his hands. "You know," he said, "this is probably the longest conversation you and I have ever had."

"So?"

He shrugged. "I'm just saying."

He lapsed into silence. Leaning against the wall, they watched the clock hands crawl around the dial. At midnight, one of the doctors came to find them. "We've stopped the bleeding." The man looked tired. "She's weak, but she's stable for the moment. You should go home and get some rest."

When the doctor had gone, Heather said, "I'm going to stay."

Lee yawned. "There's nothing we can do," he said. "We should both get some sleep."

"Even so."

"No, come on." He pulled out his mobile. "I'm going to call my driver. I can give you a lift home. You need to check on Lewis. He'll need you, and Kerri's asleep anyway. Let me take you home, and I'll send the car back for you in the morning. You can get a good night's sleep and still be back here when she wakes up tomorrow."

Heather looked around at the crowded plastic seats and the clusters of half-empty coffee cups. The place stank of disinfectant, sweat and impatience. In the opposite corner of the room, a cleaner mopped around the feet of relatives waiting for news of loved ones.

"Okay," she said.

•

She followed him out onto the street. The rain had stopped, and a watery moon shone through veils of orange cloud. Lee turned up his collar.

"I can get her transferred to a private hospital."

Heather shook her head. She fumbled in her bag for her umbrella. "No, she wouldn't want that."

"Because it's me?"

"Partly." Heather smiled despite herself. "Also, she doesn't believe in private healthcare."

Lee's phone rang. It was the driver. Some sort of disturbance was going on, and he couldn't get close to the hospital. The roads were blocked.

"Wait there," Lee told him. He pocketed the phone and turned to Heather. "We'll have to walk a little way, I'm afraid."

She tugged the strap of her bag more firmly onto her shoulder. "Whatever."

Side by side, they made for the Euston Road, their footsteps loud on the quiet pavements. The air felt fresh and clean after the closeness of the waiting room. An airliner passed overhead; its red and green lights winked.

"It's just a plane," Lee reassured himself. Beside him, Heather raised an eyebrow.

"What did you say?"

"Nothing." They were nearing the Tube station. Ahead, he could hear the restless grumble of a crowd. Blue lights glanced off the wet-slicked tarmac. A glass bottle smashed.

Heather slowed. "Maybe we should go another way?"

"No, come on." All Lee wanted was to get to his car, and then back to his hotel. They emerged onto the main road. The carriageway had been closed to traffic. At one end, a phalanx of armed police faced off against an agitated mob.

"I don't like this," Heather said.

Lee was too tired to care. He'd seen similar protests in other cities. Wherever the Reefs sprang up, unrest followed. Some wanted to purge the infection, others to embrace it. He took her hand and began walking in the direction of the police lines. He could see his car, waiting on the curb a hundred metres or so behind the farthest riot van. All he had to do was flash his ID when they reached the front ranks of riot policemen, he thought, and they'd be through; but, as they drew closer, he heard a roar of voices behind him, the sound of running feet. Looking back, he saw the crowd surging forwards; placards and sticks held aloft, mouths screaming open, faces contorted, stones and other missiles raining from their hands. A Molotov cocktail arced overhead and shattered on the road between Lee and the waiting constabulary. He got a waft of heat, a whiff of petrol. Heather tried to drag him into a doorway, but they were caught up with the rioters now, driven forward like fishing boats running ahead of a storm, unable to fight the current for fear of getting capsized and trampled.

Ahead, the police sheltered behind a line of riot shields. Their faces were shadowed beneath helmets and visors. They waited until the crowd was almost within touching distance, and then let fly with a volley of gunfire. Lee heard the flat, echoing reports, saw the smoke. Someone went down to his left. He heard cries. The frontrunners tried to slow but were pushed on by the weight of those behind.

Another volley.

Heather jerked and fell. Her fingers slipped from his.

The charge broke up. Only the foolhardiest continued to storm the impregnable shield wall. The rest ran from the shots, barging into and tripping over each other in their hurry to get away, to put something solid between themselves and the projectiles loosed by the police.

Lee found Heather lying on her side in the street. She had been kicked and trodden upon. A bloody red welt disfigured her forehead, and her eyes had rolled up into their sockets, showing only the whites through half-closed lids. A plastic bullet lay beside her, the end rimed in crimson. He knelt beside her on the wet road. The baton round had hit the front of her skull like a spoon hitting the top of a boiled egg. Her mouth hung slack, and a line of drool trailed from the corner of her lip. Rain pooled in her open eyes. Without knowing why, he picked up the plastic bullet that had killed her. It felt warm in his hand, like a sun-warmed rock on the lip of a Welsh quarry.

Thunder rolled.

The rain grew heavier.

Lee knelt there, cradling the bullet in his hand, until the police came to take him away.

6.

Lee stood on his balcony and looked out over the grey waters of the Thames. From here, near Waterloo Bridge, he could see the Gherkin and the dome of St. Paul's in one direction, and the London Eye and the Houses of Parliament in the other. The view gave him a sense of crawling satisfaction. It made him feel close to the centre of things, perched at the intersection of politics, religion and commerce. Recently, some of his friends had taken their fortunes and moved out to large houses in Oxfordshire or the Cotswolds; but he never would. He couldn't imagine himself living in the countryside again. He needed light and noise. Going back would feel like a return to his childhood on the Welsh border, where it was always too quiet at night and the rolling hills held too many ghosts. He took a sip of orange juice from the wineglass in his hand. Out on the river, a pleasure barge sounded its foghorn. A plane rumbled through the overcast sky. A train pulled out from Waterloo Station, rattling and clattering its way across the bridge.

"Thank you," he said.

Beside him, Edward Harrell placed his own half-empty glass on the balcony rail and adjusted his cufflinks.

"No thanks necessary." He was a portly man with a flushed face and thick, florid lips. He wore a pinstripe three-piece suit and shiny black brogues. His fingers were short and thick like expensive sausages. "I even spoke to the PM, and she's been very impressed. Especially with the way you handled that business in the Mediterranean. Not to mention the incident in Cornwall."

Lee shrugged. "We lost good men in both those operations."

"But, in each case, you prevented an outbreak."

"And that's why you're offering us this contract?"

Harrell leant on the rail. The wind ran a comb through his thinning hair. "Essentially, yes. You're doing a good job rounding up the infected, but if we're going to really contain this thing, we're going to have to be ruthless." Lee looked down at the remaining juice in his glass.

"And you think we're the right company for the job?"

Harrell smiled. "We do."

"But these camps you've set up..."

"Purely a precautionary measure. We hand over the running of them to your security personnel, and they keep the inmates confined until we're sure they haven't been infected."

"And how long will that be?"

"We don't know."

Spots of rain began to fall, borne on the wind. Lee led his guest back inside, into his study. The floors were polished hardwood; the rugs were from Morocco; a Swedish recluse had designed the furniture. A brass telescope stood on a tripod beside the door. Tasteful picture frames held photographs of Lone Tower's space launch facilities in North Africa: rocket gantries silhouetted against the rising sun; platinum missiles hurling themselves into the wide, blue desert sky.

"And what happens to the infected?"

"They'll be euthanized and incinerated."

Lee swallowed. "I'm not sure I'm entirely comfortable with this."

Harrell eased himself into an armchair. "There's no reason not to be. This is purely a security contract. It's just like guarding young offenders or illegal immigrants. You keep them detained and you process them. If they're clean, they leave by the front door; if they're infected…"

Lee felt a shiver at the back of his neck. "What?"

Harrell blew into his fist and opened his fingers, miming smoke. "They leave via the chimney."

Lee's stomach tightened. On unsteady legs, he walked around and took a seat behind his desk. Picking up a pen, he tapped the end nervously against the palm of his opposite hand. "I'll have to think about it."

The other man's jowls settled around his collar like candle wax around the top of a cheap restaurant wine bottle. "In which case, I'd have to advise you to think quickly. We won't ask twice."

Outside, the rain thickened, falling like static from a monochrome sky. It splashed onto the wooden decking of the balcony, and into Harrell's abandoned wineglass, diluting the remaining orange juice.

"What's in it for me?"

Above the sound of the rain, Lee heard pots clatter in the kitchen. Kerri and Lewis had been staying with him for the past fortnight, since Kerri's release from hospital. With Heather dead and her assets in the hands of her inhospitable family, they had nowhere else to go.

Harrell sniffed. "Have you ever considered politics, Mr. Doyle?"

A plane whined overhead. Lee placed the pen on the desk and pushed back in his chair. The casters whispered on the wooden floor.

"I'm just a software engineer." His modesty was a default response, one he often used as a way of evading questions. Harrell didn't fall for it.

"Decide quickly," he said. "And perhaps, while I'm waiting, you could offer me something a little stronger than fruit juice?"

Lee stumbled to his feet. He glanced at the mantelpiece, where a smooth pebble sat between framed photographs and plastic trophies—a prize gathered by Lewis on a trip to Brighton the day before, and the first and only gift Lee's son had ever given him. "Of course."

He walked over to the drinks cabinet and reached for the scotch. As he poured, his heart hammered against the lining of his chest. He'd lost his wife in an avalanche the night the Reefs first came; almost lost Kerri in an outbreak. If further losses were to be avoided, something had to be done. Lone

Tower squads had been rounding up changelings for months now. Several had already died in custody and been quietly vivisected in the corporation's laboratories, the secrets of their rewritten DNA funnelled into a hundred research and development projects. Taking control of the camps would merely be a way of formalizing the process, only this time with government backing. The potential rewards—both in terms of finance and science—were staggering. One of the changelings recovered from the Cornish debacle had been perfectly adapted to life underwater, with gills, webbed appendages, and a vastly increased lung capacity. Suppose somewhere, one of the Reefs spat out a human being capable of surviving in space without expensive air tanks and pressure suit? He could barely imagine how much something like that would be worth.

"Sod it," he said, letting his accent slip. "I'm in. The shareholders would kill me if I walked away from a government contract." He passed one of the drinks to Harrell, who enfolded it in meaty fingers.

"So, you'll do it?"

Lee bit his lip. He knew he was doing the right thing, the responsible thing; yet still felt as if he was about to agree to something huge, dark and irrevocable. He knocked back the whisky from his glass and swallowed hard. The fumes made his eyes water. "Yes."

•

Three days later, they came for Kerri. A Lone Tower security squad pulled into the car park of his building in an armoured troop carrier with blacked-out windows and Lone Tower logos on its sides. There were five of them, and they all carried assault rifles. Waving a signed court order, they simply walked through Lee's bodyguards, who found themselves outgunned and legally outmanoeuvred.

When they came through the front door of his apartment, Lee blocked their path. "Do you know who I am?"

"Yes sir. But there are to be no exceptions."

"I could fire you right here, right now."

"Wouldn't do any good, sir. We're hired through a subcontractor. You'd have to take it up with them."

Two of the men restrained him while the other three marched Kerri from the building. Her hands were cuffed but her chin remained high and defiant as if, somehow, she'd always known this would happen. Lewis kicked and screamed for his mother. Lee held him back as the doors slammed and the truck drove away. As it vanished from sight, the boy twisted in his grip and buried his face in Lee's shoulder.

"It's okay." Lee put a hand to the back of the kid's head.

"No, it isn't." Lewis's fingers clawed at Lee's shirt. "You let them take her." He pulled away, features screwed up like a fist, an index finger held out in shaking accusation. "You're a monster. You let them take her. You let them." He turned and ran. "I hate you; I hate you; I hate you!"

7.

The limousine emerged from the underground garage, nosing its way through shouts and placards. Hands banged the windows. Feet kicked the bodywork. It pulled out into the street and a shoe hit the rear windscreen. Then they were clear and moving through the city. On the back seat, Lee Doyle loosened his tie and undid the top button of his shirt. Despite their hatred of him, he couldn't summon any animosity towards the protestors. Let them shake their handwritten signs and shout their slogans. They weren't his problem anymore; he was leaving, and he was taking Lewis with him. Looking through the smoked glass window at the black taxis and red buses, he knew these moments in the car were the last he'd ever spend in London with his son, so he tried to drink it all in with his eyes—the tourists and pigeons flocking together in Trafalgar Square; the brick-faced pubs and narrow side streets; the bus stops and Underground stations. He tried to stuff it all into his head so he'd never forget; so, he could carry it with him on the journey ahead.

Beside him, hunched up against the far door, Lewis had plugged into his tablet. He had his earphones in, mainlining aggressive skater music. He hadn't spoken since the ride began and had barely looked up from the screen. The past few days had been tense for them both, and Lee preferred this silent treatment to the usual tantrums and shouting.

Between them on the seat, a locked steel briefcase held Lee's few remaining possessions: some personal papers; an old USB memory stick; a gold pen; some sheep's wool; a gold ring; a lump of clear Perspex containing a single Alpine snowflake; a plastic bullet; the pebble his son had given him; and enough money to get them where they were going. He'd had to abandon everything else. He'd left his penthouse apartment unlocked and his Porsche on a South London street with the windows open and the key in the ignition. His stock portfolio had been signed over to a children's charity and his modern art collection donated to the National Gallery. Beside his son, the only things that mattered to him were the items in the briefcase and the clothes he wore.

Following instructions, the driver took them out along the A40, towards Oxford. Lee had a helicopter standing-by at a private airfield near High Wycombe. By the time they got there, it was fuelled and ready to depart.

At the cabin door, he paused to take a last breath of England. The air smelled of hot concrete, aviation fuel and cut grass. Inside the cabin, he tried to help Lewis strap in, but the boy shook him off. The kid didn't want his help; didn't even want to be here. Lee had pulled him from school without notice, against the protestations of the staff. Now, they were the only passengers. Through the small window at his elbow, he saw the limo retreating. The driver had been well paid and meticulously briefed; the car would be found the following morning, abandoned in a service area close to the Severn Bridge with Lee's handwritten suicide note pinned to the centre of its steering wheel. A pair of his favourite shoes and a gold Rolex would be found on the bridge itself, as if discarded by their owner. Lee rubbed his face with his hands. If his ruse worked, he and his son would be presumed drowned, their bodies washed out to sea on the estuary's tide.

Overhead, the rotors were turning. Lee closed his eyes and imagined the hardness of sun-warmed stone blocks, the smell of sheep shit and fresh grass, and the thudding downdraught of an army chopper wending its way southwards, following the river down the length of a Welsh valley. He squeezed the armrests. Memories were forged iron links, fettering him to the past. The only way to smash free was to become somebody else, to shed his past like a spent ammo clip and take on a new identity. As the tarmac fell away and the greys of the airfield shrivelled into the green and yellow squares of the Buckinghamshire countryside, he imagined crumpling his life in his hand like a discarded, half-written letter.

Goodbye, Lee Doyle.

Fall away in the downdraught.

•

His phone rang as the helicopter crossed the inundated coast between Portsmouth and Chichester. "Yes?"

"Mister Doyle? It's George Tyson."

"Who?"

"Bullock's man."

"What do you want?" Lee looked out of the rain-streaked cabin window. They were so low the helicopter's skids almost kissed the water; its rotors whipped spray from the granite grey swell.

"We found her, sir."

Lee's heart seemed to pause in his chest. "Where is she?"

"The camp on Anglesey."

"Can we get her out?"

"We're already trying."

He let out a long breath and wiped his free hand across his mouth. He had scarcely dared believe she would still be alive. "Have her taken to the launch facility."

"I'll see to it." The man gave a polite cough. "And sir?"

"Yes?"

"I think you'd better take a look at the news."

Lee killed the call and used his phone to access a live TV feed. The pictures were the same on all the channels. The British army had stormed into the Lone Tower quarantine camp and research facility on Salisbury Plain, and the resulting footage had gone viral. At first, Lee tried to shield his son's eyes from the images; but when the boy struggled, he gave up. He didn't have the strength to resist. All he could do was watch in horror as the soldiers tried to help the emaciated prisoners. A shaking cameraman walked around the lip of one of the 'tanks'—the large metal rooms where prisoners were systematically drowned, and their skeletons bleached to kill off any lingering infection. Mounds of gleaming skulls lay in a trench out behind the building, waiting to be covered over and buried. Other trenches had already been back-filled with concrete—row upon row of them, stretching away towards the barbed wire at the camp's perimeter. Enough, the voiceover suggested, to house five thousand bodies, perhaps more.

In response, Lone Tower security personnel and scientists were being handcuffed and bundled into camouflaged lorries. In London, military police took control of the House of Commons and the government fell, live on air. Shamed politicians were led from the building with towels covering their faces. Lee Doyle, the head of the company operating and making a profit from the death camps, had been declared a fugitive and an enemy of humanity. An army spokesman promised that the new martial authority would do everything in its power to locate him and bring him to justice.

Tears running down his face, Lee watched the reports cycle over and over, the same gristly images of the camps—and the pictures of his own face— repeating in a sequence he knew would torture him, waking and sleeping, for the rest of his life.

He'd known things were bad; he'd just had no idea how bad...

Without taking his eyes from the screen, he pulled the gold pen from the briefcase. It was the same pen with which he'd signed Harrell's contract, believing he was doing something to help save humanity from the scourge of the

Reefs; the same pen he'd used to lend his stamp of approval to reports and planning documents that had eventually led thousands, maybe hundreds of thousands, of men, women and children to their deaths. He wanted to drop it, to throw it away. Instead, he closed his fist around it. He would never let it go. He would carry it with him now, wherever he went. Thanks to its gold case, it had always been a heavy pen. Now, clasped in his hand, its weight was almost more than he could bear.

•

Two hours and forty minutes after crossing the English Channel, the jet touched down at the Lone Tower launch facility in Algeria. Stepping from the plane, Lee put a hand to shade his eyes against the desert glare. Sweat broke out beneath his shirt. The heat here was an order of magnitude greater than it had been in London.

The Hammaguir facility lay in the desert southwest of Béchar. It comprised a brace of runways and a cluster of prefabricated buildings; a few Fuller domes; and a new, white-painted water tower. Heat mirages shimmered at either end of the runway. The first French satellite had been launched from here in 1965. Now, Lone Tower owned the place, and, for the past five years, had been using it to launch payloads into orbit.

Aware that he would never again ride in his private jet, Lee pocketed a small cardboard book of complimentary matches as a souvenir. The cover had the Lone Tower corporate logo printed on the front.

With Lewis in tow, he made his way across the sand-blown tarmac to the main building at the edge of the airfield, where he was welcomed by one of the project leaders, a stocky former NASA employee by the name of Constance Marcelene.

"Welcome to Algeria," she said.

Lee gave her a thin smile. The three of them were alone in the arrivals lounge. "I want three spaces on the next launch."

Connie's heavy mascara blinked at him. "Three...?"

"Me, Lewis, and one other."

The woman frowned. "But it's only seventy-two hours away. We have the crew assigned, most of the cargo loaded..."

"I don't care." Lee un-shouldered his bag and let it fall to the floor. "Do whatever it takes, but you have to get us on that flight."

Connie pursed her lips. "Things are at a crucial stage," she said. "The *Widening Gyre*'s going to leave next week, whether we've finished loading or not. With all due respect, we have neither the time nor the resources to send any more tourists up to see it."

Lee took off his jacket and draped it over his bag. "We're not tourists," he said. "We're crew."

"But, sir-"

"No." He held up a hand to silence her protests. "The *Gyre* has room for a hundred thousand sleepers. So far, we've filled less than fifteen percent of the available pods. You'll find some way to fit us in."

•

The following evening, an ancient twin-propeller cargo plane brought Kerri to Hammaguir. Sprung from the camp, she had been smuggled out via Dublin and Morocco. Now, she remained on the plane until it had been towed into the privacy of an empty corrugated iron hangar, and the flight crew had been dismissed.

The prefabricated hangar doubled as a motor pool, and housed a couple of jeeps, a motorbike, a workbench covered in tools, and half a dozen jerry cans of unleaded petrol. Lee closed the doors and climbed the stairs into the plane. He hadn't shaved and had discarded his business suit for a black polo shirt and a pair of Bermuda shorts. The shirt had a mission badge embroidered on the left breast: a lumpy black potato ringed by two dazzling white moons. Thus attired, he could blend in among the other astronaut hopefuls kicking their heels at the base, waiting for their chance to ride into orbit on a pillar of fire.

As far as the rest of the world was concerned, the *Widening Gyre* was an orbital refuge for plant seeds and samples of animal DNA; a vault protecting them from any calamities that might befall the Earth; a cosmic back-up for the biosphere. Only a select few knew its true purpose and origin: that a Reef had created the huge ship in order to ferry humans to another star.

Equipped with its own onboard artificial intelligence, the ship set its own agenda. It would depart at a certain date, whether the humans were ready or not. So far, just over thirteen and a half thousand people had been shipped up to join the seeds and animal samples in suspended animation in its holds. By the time the world found out its true purpose—as it broke orbit and powered away from the Earth—it would be too late to stop the behemoth. If things had been different, the Americans could have theoretically intercepted the ship by repurposing one of their Martian shuttles, but Mars currently lay on the other side of the sun, some three hundred and forty-five million miles in the wrong direction. And besides, what could they do to stop it? It was simply too large and too powerful to be stopped by anything short of collision with a planet or large asteroid.

He found Kerri slumped in a wheelchair at the front of the cabin. Elastic straps held the chair in place, and her wrists had been handcuffed to its armrests. Her hair hung across her face in knotted ropes. She wore a filthy hospital gown with a number stencilled on the front. The same number had been crudely engraved into the skin of her left forearm.

"Kerri?" She didn't look up. "Kerri, it's me. It's Lee." Still she gave no answer. Her fingernails were ragged and torn, and a strange fungus-like growth disfigured the ankle and shin of her right leg. "Kerri?" He leaned down. "Can you hear me?"

"Bastard."

"What?"

She shook her wrists against their cuffs. "Bastard."

Lee straightened up. "Kerri-"

Finally, she looked at him, eyes bright and hard above taut, hungry cheekbones. "Murdering fucking bastard."

A Welsh quarry in summer. A teenage boy lay on his back, his forehead caved like the top of a boiled egg. His blood – impossibly bright, impossibly red – seeped down his temples, into his ears and hair. His feet, still encased in unlaced, dusty trainers, twitched.

"I didn't mean to." Lee's fists went to his chest. He felt sick. "I wanted to scare him. He was trying to take you away. I had to stop him."

Kerri scowled. "I'm talking about the camps." She took a ragged breath. "The lines of people filing into the swimming pools, day after day. And nobody coming back out."

"Kerri, I didn't know."

"You signed the orders."

"I thought we were doing the right thing." He ran a hand back through his hair.

"You signed the orders."

"I know, but-"

"You signed the fucking orders, Lee. It's all down to you. All of it."

Lee's fingers curled into his palms. He took a deep, pained breath. "What do you want me to say?"

Kerri's lip curled. "I don't think there's anything you can say." Her shoulders relaxed and she seemed to sag in on herself.

"But I got you out."

"No." Her eyes were focused on something else; some internal horror he couldn't see. "No, not really."

"Yes." He tried to force positivity into his voice. "Yes, look where we are. I've got you and Lewis, and I'm getting us all out of here for good."

Kerri's head twitched at the sound of her son's name. "Lewis is here?"

"Yes."

"I don't want him to see me like this."

"We'll get you cleaned up."

"No." She tugged at the cuffs manacling her to the chair. "No, it's too late for that. Keep him away. Keep them all away."

"Kerri, I'm trying to save you."

"It doesn't matter." Her breath rasped between her teeth. Her lips curled in a sneer. "Nothing you do will ever matter, because you signed those orders with that stupid gold pen of yours. You sent those people, those children, to their deaths. And you did it for money."

Her heels stamped against the chair's plastic footrest. The growth on her shin twitched. To Lee's horror and revulsion, it blossomed. He could see tendrils moving under the skin of her arms and neck and face. Blue-black buboes erupted at her knees and elbows. Charcoal froth bubbled from her dry lips. For a second, their eyes met. He saw her fear. Then Kerri tipped her head back and gave a long, raw howl; the ragged scream of a dying animal. The blackness burst from her ears and eyes. It split her skull and consumed her skin. Lee wanted to turn and run but his legs refused to move. He couldn't turn away. Within seconds, Kerri had been consumed, burned away by the Reef within, leaving only a vaguely human-shaped tower of smart matter, its roots extending down through the fabric of the wheelchair and into the metal deck of the plane.

Feeling unsteady, Lee forced himself to take a step back. As he did so, a thin string-like tentacle whipped from the base of the Reef and wrapped itself around his ankle. He yelled and tried to pull away but couldn't disentangle himself. He reached down to dislodge it, but a second tentacle flicked out to snare his wrist. Pain stabbed his temples and he cried out. He screwed his eyes against the agony—

•

And then he was elsewhere. The wind brought the scent of warm grass; the bleat of sheep; and the sound of cars down on the main road. Slowly, he straightened up and cracked his eyes against the sun's white glare. "No."

Not here. How could he possibly be *here*?

He looked up at the moss-mottled grey flank of the round ruined tower, stark against the bracken-coated hills and blue skies of youth; the rectangular fir plantations with their razor-straight edges; the unruly, jigsaw fields. Near the top of the structure, a solitary arched window stood dark and empty like a ravaged eye socket.

Like the hollow left in the chest of a boy with no heart.

Kerri was sitting in the dust, her back to the warmth of the stones, her bare feet scuffing amongst the dried grass stalks and fallen stones.

She was fourteen again.

Gone were the rags and grime of the prison camp, the lines and cares of maturity. In their place, the girl she'd been all those years ago, before that afternoon in the quarry, in the days when they had both been at their happiest and life had seemed no more than an endless August drowse.

Lee wanted to burst into tears, to prostrate himself on the baked ground at her toes and beg her forgiveness—not just for what he'd done and what he'd become, but also for the missed opportunities, the words left unspoken and paths left untaken. They'd had such teenage dreams. The world had been a bright canvas, stretching out in all directions. They would go anywhere and do everything. But, after the quarry, all that had changed. The cyst of their happiness ruptured. The wave function of endless possibility collapsed, leaving them stranded, guilty and alone, on the shores of an inhospitable puberty.

For long moments, he stood and watched her curl a finger in her stringy hair. She didn't seem to have noticed him.

Was he here at all? He felt insubstantial, ready to blow away with the thistledown.

Nervously, he coughed.

Kerri looked up with eyes that weren't the eyes of a fourteen-year-old. They were black and textured. The fabric of the Reef pushed out through her sockets, stretching the glistening film of each eye into an obscene, cancerous blister.

And yet, he knew she could see him.

He could feel her gaze and it made him feel raw and naked, exposed like a laboratory specimen pinned to a bench beneath a hot, bright light.

Blue sparks danced where her irises had once been. "Lee?"

He swallowed and bunched his fists. "No," he said. "Not anymore."

"Jason, then?"

"Yes."

Kerri's dead eyes surveyed the castle grounds. "Do you like it?"

"You know... You know what this place means."

"Of course. Why do you think I brought you here?" She stood and brushed pale dust from her denim shorts. "It's all about memories, Lee." She tapped her temple with a bitten fingernail. "You can change your name, but you can't run from what's up here."

Lee's heart thumped at the back of his throat. "Who are you?"

The teenager smiled. "I'm Kerri."

"No, you're not."

The girl shrugged. "Well, I'm also the Reef, of course. I'm both. To be honest, it's sort of hard to tell where one ends and the other begins."

Lee cocked his head at the grass and sheep. "And this place?"

The smile grew wider. "Think of it as your own personal road to Damascus."

•

An eternity later, Lee staggered from the plane, eyes watering and mind sodden with images of the camps—of the frightened men, women and children jammed like sheep into lightless shipping containers; of the dormitories that were little more than concrete huts with straw on the floor; of the flies that crawled over everything and everyone; and the constant, all-permeating smell of the bleach.

Silent and trembling, he walked down the steps from the plane. He picked up a jerry can of petrol and returned to the cabin, where the Reef stood swaying in a non-existent breeze, its tendrils investigating the surrounding seats and overhead air vents. Moving without hurry, he unscrewed the cap and emptied the fuel over the writhing black mass and the remains of the wheelchair. Then he reached into his pocket and pulled out the complimentary matchbook from his private plane.

•

Standing outside, in the full glare of the setting sun, Lee watched the hangar burn. Even from a hundred paces away, he could feel the heat of the flames on his face and hands. By the time the fire crew arrived, howling across from the far side of the airfield, the jet fuel had caught and reduced the prefabricated structure to a flaking metal furnace.

Thick, greasy smoke roiled into the azure desert sky. It stung the monster's eyes. He took a pair of mirrored aviator shades from his pocket and slid them onto his face. Then he turned on his heel and walked away.

The roof of the building crashed inward in a shower of ash and sparks, but he did not look back. The monster just kept walking across the lone and level sand.

Ahead, a white rocket glistened on its pad, vapour steaming from its cryogenic tanks.

Earth was over.

8.

Lee's first sighting of the *Widening Gyre* came as the crew module lined up for its final approach. He was strapped into a couch with his head craned against the glass of a porthole. The big ship's bulk obscured the stars like the very hand of God reaching out from the darkness. Bathed in the glow of the Earth, the *Gyre*'s skin looked a dark navy blue. The paler spots of impact craters, which gave its bow the appearance of a barnacle-encrusted whale's snout, had mottled it. The two pale moons, *Odyssey* and *Iliad*, revolved around the ship's waist like attendant ghosts, their function unknown and un-guessable. All attempts by the human crew to penetrate them had been frustrated, and the Reefs had finally asked the humans to leave the two misshapen eggs alone and concentrate instead on the business of filling the main ship's hold with as many frozen sleepers as possible.

The module carrying Lee and his son also carried another forty candidates, all volunteers. After docking, they were divided into three batches and shown to the changing rooms by a red-suited orderly with a handheld palmtop. Lee and

Lewis were put into separate groups and led to different rooms.

"Find your locker," the orderly said, "and disrobe. When you're ready, go through that door and find your designated berth."

•

"Jason Pembroke." However many times he said it, it still felt strange. As far as history would be concerned, Lee Doyle had died almost a week ago, after jumping from the Severn Bridge, and his body had been lost to the Bristol Channel tide. Only Pembroke remained—a man who, although less sure of himself, resembled in the right light an unshaven, red-eyed and hollow-cheeked facsimile of the disgraced CEO.

Standing in front of his locker, in the tiled changing rooms, Lee unzipped his flight suit and bundled it into the waiting plastic bag. He slipped off his shoes and, after a quick look around to make sure everyone else was doing likewise, stripped off his socks and underwear and bundled them all into the locker.

The air on his skin felt cool and strangely invasive. He hadn't been naked in public since... He scratched his head. Had he ever been naked in public? There had been that time at University, during the Hay Literary Festival, when he'd gone skinny-dipping with two friends in the River Wye, but he wasn't sure if that counted as being 'in public', as the only witnesses had been half-a-dozen bemused cows.

Some of the other members of the group were talking, exchanging nervous jokes and laughing at their own self-consciousness. Arms and legs prickling with gooseflesh, Lee pretended to rearrange the contents of his locker. He wanted to let them go first. Even at this late stage, he was worried he might be recognised and returned to Earth. A lot of these people had been Lone Tower employees, and many were fleeing the company's slow implosion following the revelation of the existence of the camps. He could trust some of them, but not all, and he didn't know how they'd react to finding him suddenly— nakedly—amongst them. As they filed through into the chill gloom of the vault beyond, he retreated barefoot to the white-tiled toilet cubicles.

How had everything gone so wrong in his life? How had it all fallen away?

Standing in front of a row of sinks, he considered himself in the mirror, searching the flat coins of his eyes for some sort of explanation—some trace of the lonely young boy who'd once pictured himself as the last scholar in a world of barbarians, alone in a tower of musty books.

Could he have saved Kerri? The sudden doubt slid its way into his gut like a cold stiletto. Had she still been alive when he poured on the petrol? He gripped the sides of the sink. What did it matter? What was one more death compared to the thousands who'd died in the camps? So many that their stacked and bleached remains lost all trace of individuality and their skulls became piles of repeating motifs, like a Warhol painting rendered by Bruegel. He leant forward until his forehead kissed the mirror. His insides were a fist and he could taste bile at the back of his throat.

His first heave brought up the remains of the black coffee that had served him as breakfast. When he heaved a second time, he felt a weight shift inside. Something small and heavy pushed its way up his oesophagus. He couldn't breathe. He was chocking. In desperation, he gave a final tortured retch. The thing scraped his teeth and fell into the sink with a loud clank.

Lee's knees sagged and he had to hold onto the sides of the basin for support.

"Shit," he gasped, "shit, shit."

He grabbed a paper towel from the dispenser beside the sink and used it to wipe his eyes and mouth.

Sitting in the plughole, surrounded by a lukewarm puddle of watery coffee, sat a small metal sphere about the size of a Ping-Pong ball, sticky and glistening with blood and mucus.

•

When Lee returned to the changing rooms a few minutes later, they were deserted. The lockers were closed. All the other sleepers had gone through to the vault and were probably already ensconced in their caskets, if not already in hibernation.

He held the metal ball in his fingers as if cradling a precious egg or an unstable explosive. It must have been implanted in his stomach while he was 'inside' the Reef, talking to Kerri. But what was it? If the Reef wanted to absorb him, it could have done so at the time. All he could think was that this heavy little nugget must represent some sort of seed, that the Reef was using him as a way of reaching into space and that, when the *Widening Gyre* finally reached its destination, a rocky little world in the habitable zone of Gliese 667 C, it would flower.

His heart rattled like a tin mug against the bars of a Louisiana jail.

Was it possible this seed also contained Kerri's memories? When the Reef had spoken to him, it had told him that her personality had become inextricably entwined with its own artificial consciousness. Could this little ball hold a record of everything she'd been, everything she'd done? He could almost feel the weight of her life in his palm. Aside from Lewis, it was all he had left of her.

Coming to a sudden decision, he crossed to his locker, opened his memory box, and placed the ball inside. When he closed the lid, her memories and his were left to nestle together in the darkness.

Swallowing down the sour taste in his mouth, he opened the door to the main vault. Now, all he had to do was adjust the controls of his hibernation pod, to get it to revive him halfway through the ship's flight. As Lee Doyle was the owner and CEO of Lone Tower, the company responsible for outfitting this outlandish vessel, he knew there would be plenty of information about him stored in the ship's memory—information that could potentially identify Jason Pembroke as a fraud. Until that information was wiped, he would never be able to relax. He would spend the rest of his life living like a former Nazi on the run in South America, always half-expecting discovery and prosecution for his crimes. The only way he would ever feel safe, ever have a hope of making a new start on the new world, would be to wake while everybody else was still in hibernation, and expunge the records himself.

9.

A decade after the *Widening Gyre* bade farewell to the blue marble of the Earth, Lee awoke in his pod. As he opened his eyes, the last of the cryogenic gel had already drained from the container and the lid yawned open, leaving him wet and naked in the cold air of the vault.

He sat up slowly.

For a few moments he couldn't remember who he was. Then he recalled the dense metal ball he'd puked into the sink.

A burning aircraft hangar.

Hollow-eyed skulls heaped beside an earthen trench.

With a small curse, he gripped the sides of the tank and pulled himself out. Although his head felt foggy and thick, he knew who he was now, and everything that entailed.

Without pausing to look at the other sleepers, he made his way out, through the changing rooms, to the corridor beyond.

"Do you need assistance?" Mi Sun, the ship's controlling intelligence, spoke to him via a fly-sized drone. "Has your hibernation capsule malfunctioned, Mister Pembroke?"

Lee swiped at the drone with the back of his hand. "Buzz off."

He pushed his way through a pair of double doors, into the room that housed the cupola.

He couldn't just instruct the computer to wipe sections of its own memory. There were safeguards preventing accidental and criminal data loss, and to try would leave a record of both what was deleted, and who deleted it. The only way to make sure he remained undiscovered would be to destroy all evidence—and the only way to do that was to inflict catastrophic damage on its main memory core.

Of course, he knew his plan entailed a certain degree of risk. Mi Sun controlled everything aboard the ship, from the engines to the life support, but he reckoned he could trash her memories without compromising her functionality. Her memories were centralised on a single server, but the life support systems were distributed on smaller servers throughout the ship. All he had to do was get into the room below the cupola and find the right server in the ship's smart matter core.

He let the fly trail him down to the main hangar, where he entered one of the ground-to-orbit shuttles and retrieved a set of tools intended for use in the building of a new world.

"What are you doing with those?"

Lee unclipped the lid and, ignoring the hammers, saws and wrenches contained within, pulled out a handheld blowtorch. "Go away."

Gripping the torch like a gun, he descended to the cavern housing the computer's memory banks. There were locks on the door but, as they had been supplied by Lone Tower, his thumbprint overrode them. It was a back door he'd built into all the company's tech, right from the earliest days. Whatever Lone Tower produced; Lee Doyle could access.

In the centre of the room, Mi Sun's smart matter memory dump looked like a row of pyramids made of hard, black plastic. They were built of the same material as the Reefs—for an instant, he felt nauseous, recalling the way Kerri had been ripped apart and consumed in the aeroplane—but he had been assured that limitations had been imposed, preventing the kind of runaway expansion that characterized those entities.

"You shouldn't be in there," Mi Sun said from the other side of the door. The nose of the drone tapped against the safety glass panel like a bee caught against a summer window. Lee ignored her. As far as he knew, Reefs were flammable. At least, he knew that in the past, flamethrowers and napalm had been used to sterilize them. This core was built from the same stuff they were. All he had to do was burn the server continuing the crew records. The computer would be lobotomized, but other servers, controlling the life support and engines, would still function. All records from Earth would be gone, and he would be Jason Pembroke—just one anonymous crewmember amongst thousands.

He made his way along the row until he came to what he thought was the correct server. Holding the torch in front of him, he depressed the trigger. Flame roared, blue and narrow. Where it touched, the black matter flared orange and white. It shrivelled away from the heat, throwing off acrid plastic fumes. Behind him, he heard the tiny drone banging against the door.

"Stop it!" The computer's voice actually sounded alarmed.

Lee laughed. He was burning his past, imagining it all crisping and curling and disintegrating into ash.

Death to it all! Death to the valleys and the attic room in Hotwells; death to guilt and regret; to every stupid, lazy decision that had ever led him here. Death to the monster Lee Doyle!

•

He played the flame into the melting pyramid until he'd exhausted the gas cylinder in the handle. Overall, he'd burned a crater roughly the width of a manhole cover, and the depth of his forearm. At the bottom, embers smouldered like sunset clouds, giving the black pyramid the appearance of a stylised volcano.

Had he done enough damage?

The ship's drone had stopped banging against the glass. When he opened the door, he found it lying inert. He bent down to pick it up.

Nothing. To all intents and purposes, it was dead, which meant the computer had shut down its higher functions. The fact the lights were still on showed its automatic systems were still online and his gamble had paid off.

Now, all he had to do was get back to his pod before the system managed to reboot itself.

Bare feet slapping the stone floors of the corridors, he returned the blowtorch to the shuttle in the hangar, and then made his way back to the vault. *En route*, he passed a large, circular window and slowed for a moment. He was out among the stars, on his way to a world around a star called Gliese 667 C, twenty-two light years from Earth. And they'd already covered a sizeable fraction of that distance. Earth, he realised, was a dot so small that, even if he knew where to look, he wouldn't be able to see it. Everything he'd done back there was gone. Everyone he'd ever known thought he was dead. All the records on the ship had been expunged. Only Jason Pembroke remained: a guy in his fifties, standing naked before the universe.

It felt like being reborn.

A movement caught his eye. He glanced upward and thought he saw, for the merest fraction of a second, the flying saucer that had appeared to him on that roadside in Somerset, all those years ago, on the evening he found out about his father's cancer. By the time he realised it was there, it had already gone, evaporating like a dream on waking, leaving only the faintest afterimage. He smiled at the space where it had been. "Goodbye, old friend."

·

As Lee settled back into his tank, he felt a surge of triumph. He'd done it. He'd screwed up his life, but he'd escaped. He'd covered his tracks. Now, he had a real chance of carving out a new existence for himself and his son, on a new frontier, on a planet so far from Earth that it took light two decades to cross the intervening distance.

The fire in the computer room still smouldered, but he was confident the ship's emergency systems would stop it from spreading. After all, he hadn't done that much damage. He'd simply performed a little surgery, burning away all evidence of his past life, along with the records of his fourteen thousand shipmates.

He smiled as liquid gel gurgled into the tank, pooling around him, and the breathing tube extruded from the wall, blindly questing for his face. When he awoke, the fire would be out, and an electrical fault would be blamed. None of the crew would know who he was, and he'd be free to reinvent himself any way he chose. He might keep the name Jason, or he might find a new one. In the meantime, all he had to do was close his eyes and hope the lingering guilt of Doyle's life evaporated while he slept.

No more Lee; no more Kerri.

No more dead boy in a summer quarry. Only Jason.

10.

THE MONSTER DIDN'T DREAM.
At least, he didn't remember dreaming.
He wasn't aware of time passing.
And when he awoke, he was already drowning.

Submerged in darkness, lungs ready to burst, he thrashed around, but the thick, warm slime had already forced its way into his nose and throat. It burned as it went down. He couldn't open his eyes. His flailing hands struck the smooth plastic walls of the vat and his panicked feet kicked against its base.

A coffin!
They were drowning him in a coffin!
He gagged. His fingers clawed and scrabbled for purchase, but the lid wouldn't move. He wanted to cry out, but he was being smothered. He couldn't breathe. The water roared in his ears. The agony in his chest swelled until it threatened to rip its way out through his ribs.

Let me out!
His fists battered the lid above him.

Why are you doing this?

The muck tasted rank and salty in his throat, like the water from an unclean fish tank. He gagged again, stomach muscles convulsing as his diaphragm spasmed. Even though his eyes were shut, he could see sparks.

Why was this happening?

His limbs felt as if they were pushing through treacle. The need to breathe was turning him inside out, and he knew he couldn't hold on. He knew he was going to die.

Just not yet.

He clamped his jaw so hard he feared his teeth would splinter.

Not yet...

His body tried to retch. His limbs thrashed. Every pulse thumped like a drumbeat. And then, just as he was on the verge of giving up – of surrendering himself to the dreadful, choking darkness – a blue light punctured the green murk. The fluid trembled to an electrical hum, and the lid above him hinged upwards, dripping.

Frantic, the monster grasped the vat's slippery lip and hauled himself up, spluttering, into coldness, light and sweet, sweet air.

•

He found himself sitting waist-deep and naked in an open vat of goo about the size and shape of a large bath. Somewhere, an alarm rang but, at first, all he could do was cough and retch, and blow wads of gunk from one nostril then the other. When he could breathe again, he wiped his eyes and tried to take stock of his surroundings.

He was in some sort of dimly lit vault that reminded him of a cinema with the lights turned down low. Other vats surrounded him on all sides. Like his, they had been inlaid so that their lips were level with the floor. Row upon row, they receded into the gloom, ascending in steps like the seats in an auditorium. Unlike his, their lids were still all in place and covered by thin patinas of frost. His breath misted in front of him. Apart from the mournful chime of the distant alarm, the only sounds he could hear were the gentle whispers of the air conditioning and the noises made by the liquid around him as it slopped in the vat when he moved.

Was he in hospital? He rubbed his forehead. There was a blank space where his memories should have been – a void, a hiss on the tape, a glitch in the program. He didn't know where he was and, with mounting panic, realised he didn't even know who he was. Even his name had gone.

He swallowed hard. He had to get out and find help. He took a fresh grip on the sides of his vat and pulled himself from the liquid's sucking embrace. Standing, the stuff came up to his knees. When he stepped up, out of the tank, his toes curled against the chill metal floor and gooseflesh prickled his calves and thighs. The air smelled cold and sterile like the inside of a fridge. The vat yawned open like a grave behind him. He needed to find a doctor or nurse, somebody to tell him what was going on, and what was wrong with him. "Hello?"

No answer came. Hugging himself and shivering, he made his way along the row of sunken, frozen caskets. Through the transparent lid of each, he could see a shadowed, sleeping form within. "Anybody?"

He left gloopy-wet footprints behind him. Every few paces, he had to stop to hawk and spit phlegm onto the floor.

Was this a morgue? Were those vats filled with the preserved dead?

At the end of the row, he came to some stairs, which led him down to the floor of the 'auditorium', to a thick metal door of the kind he imagined you'd find on a submarine. A chrome wheel opened the door. He tried to turn it the wrong way. His arms felt weaker than they should have done. When the wheel got stuck, he cursed through chattering teeth and hauled it back in the opposite direction.

Right tight, left loose. Somebody had taught him that once, but he didn't know who it might have been, or when.

After a few rotations, the wheel clunked to a stop and the lock disengaged. The door swung inwards. After the gloom of the vault, he had to shade his eyes against the light from within.

"Hello?" He could hear the alarm more clearly now. The walls and floor were tiled in white. Lockers lined the centre of the room. If you added the smell of chlorine, this could have been the changing room of a public swimming baths anywhere in the world. The air in this room was warmer than in the vault, though, and triggered a fresh bout of shivering.

He needed to find some clothes.

Each of the lockers had a number, and a hand-shaped scanner set into its door. He worked his way along the row, mashing his fingers and palm against each one in turn. On the nineteenth attempt, the scanner accepted his handprint and the locker door clicked open. Inside, he found a towel and a set of shrink-wrapped clothes hanging from a hook. He took the towel and used it to dry the worst of the goo from his skin and hair, then picked the package out. Inside the polythene was a blue one-piece overall in tough, durable cotton, with a coloured mission patch sewn onto the left shoulder and some sort of logo sewn onto the right. The nametag on the breast read, 'Pembroke, Jason. The writing on the mission patch appeared to be in French. Hands shaking, he tore off the thin plastic covering and lets it fall to the tiled floor. He didn't bother looking for underwear. Instead, he threaded his feet through the legs of the suit, wriggled his arms into its sleeves, and pulled the zipper up as far as it would go. The wrists and ankles had Velcro cuffs, and he fastened these as well. Then he stood straight and tried to control his breathing. Clothed, he felt less vulnerable and more in control. His chest and throat hurt, and he kept coughing up scraps of green vat gunk, but at least he was alive.

The mirror on the inside of the locker door showed the reflection of a middle-aged man: a few grey hairs; nothing he recognised.

"Jason Pembroke," he said aloud. The name meant nothing. It didn't feel familiar on his tongue and he wasn't even sure how to pronounce it. Should the end of the surname rhyme with crook or croak? He repeated it a few times, trying each variation, and then shrugged.

The only other items left in the locker were a pair of soft-soled shoes and a wooden box. He slipped the shoes over his half-frozen feet, and carefully lifted out the box. The word, 'MEMORIES' had been sprayed across the lid in military stencil. He opened it and frowned at the objects inside—a scrap of sheep's wool; an old USB memory stick; a gold ring; a lump of clear Perspex; something which he suspected might be a used plastic bullet; a pebble; a silver ball bearing; and a gold pen. He stirred them with his index finger, trying to decode meaning from their jumble.

Something's badly wrong, he thought. The alarm was still ringing, but he could hear no voices, no running feet. A hospital shouldn't have been this deserted, even at night. And then there was the fact that he'd almost drowned. He clenched his jaw. How the hell had that been allowed to happen? And what were those tanks, anyway? What were those people doing in them, and why were they submerged?

He snapped the box's lid shut and made for the door at the far end of the changing room. It opened onto a wide corridor. Perhaps, if he could make his way to an exit, he could get out into the street and find someone who could tell him what was going on. But which way should he turn? There weren't any windows; no clues as to which floor he was on. Not even an emergency exit sign.

He coughed and spat, and, still carrying the wooden box in his hands, set off to the left. Somebody had once told him that the key to solving a maze was to keep turning left. He didn't know how true that was, but it was better than nothing. In the land of the lost, the half-assed theory was king. If he kept turning left, he was sure he'd eventually come to a lift or some stairs, or some other means of escape.

•

The monster walked for what seemed a long time, but the only doors he passed lead into rooms identical to the one he'd just left – more changing rooms, with further vaults beyond. After a couple of hundred metres, he came to a place where the corridor walls were stained with something that looked like mildew or black mould. Water dripped from the seals around the light panels set into the roof, forming little pools on the floor. Half the lights weren't working properly. Some stuttered intermittently. Wires hung from an unscrewed wall fixture. He slowed his pace. This was starting to look less like a hospital and more like an abandoned building site. Still, he kept shuffling forwards; he didn't know what else to do.

At the end of the corridor, a pair of thick double doors blocked his path. Pushing through, he found himself in a much larger space. The corridor had become a bridge across a wide, bowl-shaped depression. A circular window had been set into the bottom of the bowl. Through its shattered remains, he could see leaping orange flames.

Something in the basement's on fire, the monster thought. Smoke trickled up through the gaps in the broken glass. It stank of burning plastic. Instinctively, he covered his mouth and nose, and, on wobbling legs, began to cross the bridge.

The few remaining panels in the circular window were coloured with abstract tessellations: fractal fern leaves interlocked in a jagged riot of flowery light, giving an effect similar to a cathedral's rose window. Above, the arching ceiling had been mirrored with thousands of silvery tiles, like an inverted disco ball. Mote-like reflections of dancing firelight speckled the walls.

When he reached the bridge's midway point, directly above the broken window, he heard a loud whoosh. The light from below snapped off. The flames disappeared, as if sucked away, and the smoke spilling from the opening stopped, and then started draining back the way it had come, whirling around the bottom of the bowl-shaped room like water leaving a bath. The monster felt the air in the chamber stir as it started to move along with the smoke. The pressure changed, and he had to swallow to pop his ears.

The air was being pulled from the room. He assumed it had something to do with the flames below consuming all the oxygen. The wind of it tugged at his clothing with insistent fingers, and he ran.

Bursting through the doors at the far end of the bridge, he gulped in a series of grateful, heaving breaths. His clothes and hair smelled like a bonfire, his lips and tongue were dry.

The building was ablaze! He had to get out!

•

On this side of the double doors, the corridor walls seemed to have been hewn from black stone. He didn't stop to admire them. Instead, he ran away from the burning room, soft shoes slapping the flagstone floor. There was another door ahead.

Oh God, he thought, *please don't let me die in a fire.*

Passing through this next door, he entered a large space filled with a knot of corrugated pipes and tubes. Water dripped from leaky joints; steam hissed. Some of the pipes were copper and pencil-thin; others were made of tough black plastic and were as wide as subway tunnels. He couldn't see the roof or the floor. A metal catwalk led him through the tangle. In places, he had to duck or even crawl.

When he reached the far end, he emerged into a large gallery: a rock- walled cavern lined with statues carved from what looked like gold. He guessed each of the sculpted figures was at least thirty feet in height. They depicted what seem to be ordinary men and women in modern clothing. They wore suits and ties, open-necked shirts and sweaters, skirts, spectacles, and wristwatches, and their stances were relaxed, almost informal. They weren't beseeching or striking heroic poses; they were simply standing companionably, oblivious to the fire alarm. Some of the figures had their hands in their pockets; some held champagne glasses. They radiated calm. In the dim light, their burnished skin seemed to glow with subtle radiance. To the monster, the effect was of being a small child at a cocktail party.

What kind of fucked-up hospital was this, anyway?

The fire alarm still rang in his ears and the scent of smoke clung to his clothes. He gripped the wooden box to stop his hands from trembling. His stomach felt like a clenched fist. Behind him, the nest of pipes hissed and gurgled. Ahead, through the thicket of golden legs, he caught sight of a window. It was round, like the smashed glass porthole he'd passed a few moments earlier, but this one looked intact, and it was set into the wall rather than the floor. Through its clear glass, he saw darkness.

Night-time, he thought, and his heart surged. That would explain why there was nobody about. As he staggered closer, he made out a handful of stars: tiny, cold points of light scattered like static against the sky.

This could be his way out. At the very least, he thought he might be able to hammer on the glass to attract attention.

When he reached it, the window was as wide across as his outstretched arms, and the glass was cold against his forehead. He looked down, expecting to see a street or parking lot, and his mouth fell open.

There were no firefighters.

There was no street.

There were no cars or buildings.

The monster's legs finally gave out and he slid down into a kneeling position. The memory box fell from his fingers and spilled its contents against the base of the window. Plastic, stone and metal objects rattled and skittered across the rock floor.

Stars lay beyond the window. Stars, and something the shape of a vast, dark rugby ball, which he now realised had always been there, waiting for him.

SPECIAL BONUS

READ THE FIRST CHAPTER OF
GARETH POWELL'S FIRST NOVEL,
SILVERSANDS

"Powell's first novel [Silversands] is a fine hi-tech romp"
– *The Guardian*

"Powell is a master ... Silversands is an excellent debut."
– *Interzone*

"A clever and, at times, brilliant novel. Powell is definitely an author to watch."
– *Morpheus Tales*

"A worthy addition to any devoted SF reader's library."
– *Suite 101*

"A great novel in a very interesting setting ... Silversands is a satisfying and enjoyable read ... Powell makes the most of his characters and backdrop to tell a page-turning story."
– *Walker of Worlds*

"Unique and exciting."
– *SFF World*

"At the forefront of science fiction."
– *SF Book Reviews*

TRANSPONDER HANDSHAKE

Avril Bradley's hands shook as she unfastened the straps holding her to her bunk. The trip through the wormhole had been rough, like a rollercoaster ride through a furnace, and she could hear the ship's heat shield creaking and groaning as it cooled. She slipped on a lightweight leather jacket and pulled her shoulder-length hair into a short ponytail. During the trip, her foil pack of cigarettes had fallen onto the deck. She picked them up and lit one, catching her reflection in the mirror above the sink. Her eyes were the pale blue of an autumn sky and her features were sharp, as if etched by the quick strokes of an impatient sculptor.

A groan came from the cabin's other bunk. It was Nina Doroshkow, the Pathfinder's middle-aged Lithuanian navigator, a tall muscular woman with a platinum crew cut and a lopsided frown.

"Do you have to smoke?" She waved a hand in front of her face. "My stomach's still doing cartwheels. This is worse than morning sickness."

"Really?" Avril took a last drag and mashed the half-finished butt into a plastic cup. To avoid straining the air recyclers, she was limited to five per day. "And exactly how many times have you been pregnant?"

"Not once." Nina smiled. "But I've heard stories. Did I tell you about my cousin? Triplets. She was sick for months."

Avril reached over and tapped the softscreen taped to the bulkhead above Nina's bunk. It brought up an external rear view. On the screen, the gate from which they'd just emerged appeared as a barely visible ring of black against the stars. It was almost impossible to judge its distance with the naked eye, but a shifting digital readout in the corner of the view showed it was slowly falling behind as the *Pathfinder*'s gentle acceleration carried them forward.

"Do you think we'll ever discover who built the gates?" Nina asked, sitting up.

Avril shrugged. It was a favourite topic of conversation amongst the crew, and everyone seemed to have his or her own pet theory. She reached into her jacket and pulled out the brooch that she habitually carried in the inside pocket. She fixed it to her collar, and then clipped her commcard to her lapel.

"Beats me," she said.

They stepped out of the cabin and made their way along the narrow gangway between the crew's quarters and the chill ranks of storage tanks where the refugees from River Fork were stored. At the end of the gangway, they took the glass elevator forward to the command deck.

The levels they passed through were ergonomic and utilitarian, laced with ducts and corridors. Decorative plants covered every available surface. Nanofilters in the ducts absorbed carbon dioxide and other toxins from the air. They passed small cargo modules holding priceless mineral samples, astronomical apparatus and cryogenically preserved samples of flora and fauna; and larger modules, which held emergency supplies and homesteading equipment.

Avril and Nina, like the rest of the crew, wore simple olive green one-piece shipsuits. Laced with nanotech, these garments could serve as pressure suits in an emergency, stiffen to provide splints for broken limbs, and store energy that could be tapped later to increase the wearer's strength. They were also capable of monitoring body functions and providing support during high-G manoeuvres. The pastel triangle of the Tanguy Corporation logo was prominent on the left breast beside the blue star insignia of the New United Nations Space Agency.

"You okay?" Nina asked.

Avril nodded and clutched the handrail as the floor of the elevator surged under them. She still felt a little sick and the uneven motion wasn't helping. "I'm just looking forward to finding out where we are."

Nina consulted her commcard. "Don't get your hopes up," she said. "According to the ship we were in the hole five and a half years this time, which means we could have travelled that many light years in any given direction."

She put a hand on Avril's shoulder and spoke in a gentler tone. "And even if we found him, it's been over sixty years since he left Earth; there's no guarantee that this man you're searching for is still alive. I've seen you disappointed twice now."

Avril shrugged her off as the elevator slowed. Her hand went to her thigh pocket and her fingers brushed the creased edge of the photograph inside, tracing the familiar cracked and curled texture. She pulled it out and smoothed the creases with her thumb. The picture was of a man in his late twenties standing on a pebbly beach. The wind ruffled his hair and chopped spray from the surf behind him. He was caught in the act of turning toward the camera, as if about to speak.

"I know," she said, tracing his face with a fingertip as the elevator doors sighed open. "But perhaps this'll be third time lucky."

•

The *Pathfinder*'s command deck was a complicated multi-level array of virtual sensor readouts and flat data screens. Nina picked up an old plastic cup from her navigation console and grimaced at the cold, curdled liquid inside. She passed it to Avril. "Better get rid of this mess before we reach turnover," she said. "We don't want it floating all over the place when we cut the thrust."

Avril dumped the cup into the recycler. "The maintenance program must have a glitch," she said, squeezing into her acceleration couch. The effects of wormhole transit were wearing off, leaving her insides feeling like a clenched fist, and her stomach growled in protest as she lit another cigarette. As she began activating the instruments on her communication console, automatic air conditioning systems cut in, unobtrusively extracting the smoke.

The first thing she opened was a damage report. Some of the ship's more delicate systems had suffered vibration damage during the transit and a couple of hull plates had buckled in the heat - but otherwise, there was nothing serious. Behind her, Mission Commander Henrik Charbonneau stepped onto the bridge, ducking to avoid the overhead screens as he edged up behind Nina's couch.

"What's our status?" he said. He had a thick French accent and his close-cropped hair was grey at the temples, adding to his natural air of grizzled authority.

"All stations report green, all crew members fully recovered from the jump," Nina said, without looking up from her monitor. "We began automatic acceleration as soon as we cleared the gate. Ship's systems are running smoothly and the medical suite reports no problems with any of the storage tanks. All sixty-seven refugees are still in suspended animation, alive if not exactly healthy."

"Have you any idea where we are?"

Nina touched a button and a revolving three-dimensional star chart appeared on one of the larger overhead screens. A jagged yellow line represented the *Pathfinder*'s course of random jumps. "From initial observations, the ship's almost one hundred per cent certain that we're here." She illuminated a star five and a half light years from Epsilon Eridani. "Tau Ceti. Nearly twelve light years from Earth. It's a main sequence, yellow-orange dwarf with about ninety per cent of the mass of Sol but only sixty per cent of its luminosity." Her voice took on a clipped, professional quality as she shifted into a routine made familiar by years of training and repetition. "We're accelerating outward from the gate at one gee. There are a couple of unremarkable gas giants on the edge of the system, and one rocky planet in the habitable zone. Estimated time of arrival: three days, fourteen hours and twelve minutes."

Charbonneau leaned over her shoulder and frowned at the displays, then spoke to Avril: "Any sign of life?"

Avril glanced down at her board. "We're picking up some radio chatter from the planet," she said. "And there's some evidence of point-to-point laser communication in the system's asteroid belt."

"Excellent." Charbonneau rubbed his hands together. "And what do we know about the planet?"

Avril called up a sub-window on the display. "It's at approximately the orbital distance of Venus. Size is point nine of Earth, mass about point nine five. The length of the year is two hundred and twenty-eight days, and the days are just under thirty standard hours. The air is thin but has a high oxygen content, which suggests the existence of indigenous life." She made an adjustment to her screen.

"And I'm picking up a signal from orbit." She frowned. "I think it's a ship."

Charbonneau narrowed his eyes. "Who are they?"

"I have access to their comm net," Avril replied. "I'm initiating transponder handshake. At this distance, it'll take about eight minutes before we get anything." She punched up the relevant menu and information flickered across the space between the *Pathfinder* and the distant transmitter.

When the reply came, she transferred the incoming data to one of the larger softscreens and began scrolling through it.

"What have we got?" Charbonneau said.

"All the usual stuff: crew and cargo manifests, ship specifications."

"Skip it. Tell me who she is."

"Aye, sir." Avril accessed the sub-channel that contained the ship's identity and flight log.

As she read, her mouth dried. She swallowed and ran a hand across her tied-back hair.

Nina looked over her shoulder and grunted in surprise. "Third time lucky," she said.

Avril laughed, still unsure if she should believe her eyes. Deep down, she'd never believed they'd find the *Anastasia*; the odds against it had been too great. But now, there on the screen, she could see the old ship's call sign.

"Do you think it's really her?" she said.

Nina leaned toward her. "Just because that's the ship he left on, it doesn't mean he's still alive," she said.

Before Avril could reply, a thin, high-pitched alarm sounded on Nina's console. The older woman slid back into position and scanned her emergency displays.

"We've got a pressure spike in one of the deuterium tanks."

"Can you control it?" Charbonneau asked.

Nina shook her head. "There's some sort of malfunction in the containment field."

"Then jettison it."

"I can't!" Nina slapped a palm against her console. "The controls are frozen. I'm completely locked out."

"Bradley!" Charbonneau barked. "Run a diagnostic. We need to trace that malfunction, fast."

"Aye, sir." Half a dozen emergency lights started blinking for Avril's attention. She pulled up enough menus to realise that whatever was causing the malfunction in the fuel containment pod was also affecting the comms system. Allowing her reflex training to guide her fingers, she opened an emergency diagnostic routine but, before she could initiate it, the whole ship shook with the force of an explosion and the lights went out.

Purchase Silversands online at Amazon

Paperback ISBN 979-8637129164
Kindle ASIN B08739GHPR

ABOUT THE AUTHOR

Gareth L. Powell was born in Bristol in 1970 and still lives nearby. He began writing at school and was fortunate to count Diana Wynne Jones and Helen Dunmore as early mentors. After a number of small press publications, he sold his first professional short story to *Interzone* magazine in 2006. A short novel, *Silversands*, appeared in 2010 and was followed a year later by his first full-length novel, *The Recollection*.

Since then, he has written many further novels, including the *Embers of War* trilogy and the four-book *Ack-Ack Macaque* series, as well as somehow finding the time to produce two short story collections, the crime novella *Ragged Alice,* and the nonfiction guide *About Writing.*

His novels have twice won the British Science Fiction Association Award for Best Novel and have been finalists for both the Locus Award in the US and the Seiun Award in Japan.

He is also the first person to have had individual work shortlisted in the Best Novel, Best Short Fiction, and Best Nonfiction categories of the BSFA Award in the same year.

Gareth has given creative writing workshops and talks at UK universities and events and has been a tutor at Arvon. He also spends a great deal of time helping aspiring authors on Twitter.

He has written nonfiction for *The Guardian, The Irish Times, SFX,* and *Acoustic Magazine,* and is a monthly columnist for *The Engineer.*

His work is published in French, German, Czech, Croatian, Italian, Russian, and Japanese, and he is represented in all professional matters by Alexander Cochran of the C&W literary agency.

Find Gareth online at
www.garethlpowell.com

Or on social media
@garethlpowell

If you enjoyed this book, please consider leaving a review or recommending it to your friends. You might also like to check out Gareth's other books on Amazon or through your local book retailer.

Printed in Great Britain
by Amazon